BLACK DAY IN NO-NAME

Caleb Black, preacher and part-time bounty-hunter, is tempted to turn in the outlaws he knows are in the ramshackle buildings he comes across. The reward money is a great incentive and he decides to go into partnership with two other black men and another bounty-hunter, Gus Spencer. Trouble is not long coming when the outlaws get wise to Caleb's scheming. Gus is badly beaten and the other three partners seem destined for Boot Hill. Will Caleb's deadly skills be enough to let them blaze their way out of danger and collect the reward money?

BLACK DAY IN NO-NAME

BLACK DAY IN NO-NAME

by

L. D. Tetlow

Dales Large Print Books
Long Preston, North Yorkshire,
England.

British Library Cataloguing in Publication Data.

Tetlow, L.D.
 Black day in No-Name.

A catalogue record for this book is
available from the British Library

 ISBN 1-85389-818-X pbk

First published in Great Britain by Robert Hale Ltd., 1997

Published in Large Print 1998 by arrangement with Robert
Hale Ltd.

Dales Large Print is an imprint of
Library Magna Books Ltd.
Printed and bound in Great Britain by
T.J. International Ltd., Cornwall, PL28 8RW.

ONE

Caleb Black weighed up the options; directly ahead but about five or six hundred feet below his vantage point on the high ridge, lay a seemingly endless plain, a carpet of various shades of brown broken by odd slashes of green, or he could continue along the trail which followed the ridge.

Crossing the plain was more-or-less in the direction he had set himself, although there was no logical reason why he should keep to that plan. He had no real idea where he was going and certainly no deadline to be anywhere. However, that direction did seem to have the advantage of being flat and therefore much easier travelling whereas following the trail seemed to mean to climb ever higher into the mountains and Caleb was not too comfortable amongst towering cliffs and steep drops into a seemingly bottomless abyss.

He studied possible ways down the steep slope on to the plain for some time and eventually and rather reluctantly decided that from where he was at that moment the descent was far too difficult and dangerous, which probably explained why the trail followed the ridge. He gently urged his horse forward along the trail hoping that he would be able to find water in the near future.

Very quickly the ridge was left behind and once again he was amongst towering bare rocks with the occasional clump of trees which at first appeared to suggest a source of water but more often did not. On the two occasions when water was to be found it proved to be most unpalatable and even his horse refused to drink it. Suddenly and most unexpectedly after about an hour during which the terrain had become thickly wooded, he came across a large pool of crystal-clear water and he could even see some quite large fish. Having been on the road for almost a week, the pool looked very inviting, even to a man who could not swim, and after unsaddling his horse and allowing her to drink her fill and turn to grazing on the lush grass, Caleb stripped off and gingerly immersed himself.

The shock was almost too much for his system; the water was almost ice cold and his first reaction was to stumble from the pool gasping for breath. After a short time though he once again braced himself and waded in. This time he was prepared and even so he gasped for breath but he was quite surprised just how quickly he became used to the temperature.

Out of the water the heat of the sun dried him off very quickly and as he slowly dressed, feeling very refreshed, his thoughts turned to food, of which he had very little—some unappetizing strips of leathery beef, a few beans, and a couple of handfuls of flour, a little salt and enough coffee to make one pot only. He sighed and thought dreamily of large steaks and fresh vegetables and apple pie. He pulled out his watch and flipped open the lid; if the watch were to be believed it was a few minutes past four in the afternoon. He looked up at the sun in the vain hope that it would tell him something different although in reality it made little difference what the position of the sun was, he had never been able to master the art of telling the time by it as some people seemed to do. He had hoped that it would be nearer noon which would have given him more time to find a town and make his dream of large steaks a reality. However, he had been living in hopes of finding civilization just around the next bend for more than a week and rather reluctantly decided that he had better stay the night where he now was.

He lit a fire and began the task of producing an unappetizing mess of the beef, beans, flour and salt, and using the last of his precious coffee. Caleb Black, Black by name and black by colour, ordained preacher and part-time bounty hunter—or should that have been bounty hunter and part-time preacher?—had to admit that whatever his talents may have been, cooking anything remotely palatable was not amongst them. He had been forcing similar messes down his throat for a good many years when it proved necessary but had never learned how to do it properly and had never really tried.

Despite it being so unappetizing he cleared his plate and drained the last of his coffee and then sat on a large rock looking down into the pool from where he could see several large fish idly swimming by and, although not a lover of fish, he found himself considering ways to catch one of them to supplement his meagre diet.

He must have been staring at the water longer than he had thought as he suddenly became aware of the light fading rapidly and once again he looked at his watch and saw that it was almost seven-thirty. He sighed and decided that it was now too late to consider catching a fish and, since even in the short time the sun had disappeared, it had become quite cold, he stoked up the fire and ensured that he had enough wood to keep it going during the night.

He had just unrolled his bedroll and had hobbled his horse before settling down for the night when he heard what was undoubtedly a shot. He sat upright and listened intently but there was no repeat shot. Now all thought of sleep had left his mind and body and slowly he made his way up a steep slope in the direction he thought the shot had come from although what he expected to see he did not know.

At first he could see nothing except vague shapes of rocks and hills, the gullies and valleys were all in total blackness, all except one more-or-less directly ahead. There were definitely several lights, all stationary and giving an impression of being very permanent and belonging to some form of established civilization.

Caleb cursed himself and then laughed. It appeared that he had just spent a few wasted hours and had resigned himself to yet another cold night under the stars when there appeared to be a town not more than a mile away. He quickly gathered his few belongings, saddled his horse and made his way along the now dark trail.

The 'town' turned out to consist of one ramshackle building which seemed to double as general store and saloon, two small barns with paddocks and three other buildings not much larger than shacks. However, if the noise issuing forth from the saloon-cum-general store was anything to go by, the population was far greater than any of the buildings could cope with. Caleb somehow had the distinct feeling that he might have been better off remaining by the lake but, since he had made his choice, he tethered his horse alongside two others in front of the saloon and, after adjusting his gunbelt and checking his two guns, he pushed aside the wing doors and marched into the dimly lit saloon. Almost immediately all conversation and the rather out-of-tune piano ceased as all eyes focused on the unexpected stranger.

A very quick mental calculation suggested that there were at least twenty other people in the room and for a few moments Caleb stood and casually looked about before finally strolling over to the counter where he ordered a beer. Surprisingly the beer turned out to be quite good and cool.

'Good evening,' said Caleb raising his glass to the staring faces behind him. 'Caleb Black at your service.'

'Ain't you some kind of preacher?' asked a voice from the darker edges of the room.

'I am,' smiled Caleb and, jokingly he thought, added, 'And I have rarely seen so many people assembled in one place who appear to need the services of a man of God so much.'

'Keep your preachin' for them as wants it!' snarled another man. 'Just keep your mouth shut, your Bible closed and your mind on your own business and we'll get along fine.'

Caleb nodded and smiled, draining his glass and ordering a refill. He was aware of two figures at his side and looked up to see two black faces staring at him. He smiled and nodded, at the same time taking in the fact that they both wore guns, but not in the fashion of experienced gunmen. Experienced gunfighters usually wore their guns slightly lower down the hip than these two did. He also wore his guns in the manner of an experienced man, but while he never attempted to hide the fact that he wore them, both were well hidden beneath his frock coat and most people seemed to assume that he did not have any.

'Good evening, brothers,' greeted Caleb. 'I never expected to see friendly faces out here.'

The man on his left grunted and lounged on the counter, his eyes on Caleb's beer, the inference obvious. Caleb smiled and indicated to the bartender that he give a beer to each of the men.

'Your good health, Padre,' said the man on Caleb's right. 'In a place like this you need all the luck and health you can get.' He raised his glass and nodded at Caleb and took a small sip.

Caleb recognized the type; a man who had served some time in prison and who now treated every drink as though it had to last for the evening, which in most cases was probably what had to happen. The fact that he had called him 'Padre' also indicated that the man had served time either in the army or prison. He also had little doubt that somewhere there was a Wanted poster which offered a reward for the apprehension of both men and, on casually surveying the other occupants of the room, Caleb could almost feel the money piling up in his pocket.

'What is this place called?' asked Caleb. 'For such a small place it sure has a lot of people. What do they all do?'

'It don't have no name,' grinned the man on his left. 'Just as most the folk here don't have no names, leastways none that they'd answer to.'

In the meantime a rather worn-out bar girl—one of three—pushed herself between the man on Caleb's right and himself and suggested that even preachers must need a bit of comfort from time to time. She was not quite so polite and friendly when he told her that this particular preacher was not interested and in any case was rather particular. She left making it clear to everyone in the room that she too was particular especially when it came to blacks. Caleb was well used to such things and ignored her.

'No name and nobody does anything,' observed Caleb. 'Somebody must do something.'

'Nobody 'ceptin' Peg-leg, he owns the place,' said the man on the left. 'My name's Royston Lockwood...' He nodded to his friend. 'This here is Ben Staples, Ben to his friends.' Caleb nodded at both but waited for further explanations. At that moment he was becoming increasingly interested in the value of the men surrounding him rather in the manner of a cattle rancher counting his livestock prior to selling them off. 'Take our advice, Padre,' continued Royston, 'get the hell out of here just as soon as you can and make sure that anythin' of value is close by you all night; there ain't one man here who wouldn't slit your throat for even a dollar.'

'Does that include you?' asked Caleb. Both men glanced at each other and then nodded. 'I'm surprised you bothered to warn me.'

'Maybe it's because you is a preacher,'

said Ben, 'and there again maybe it's because you is a black man, or maybe both. The point is, Reveren', every other man here don't give a damn about you bein' a preacher and the fact that you is black don't go down too well in your favour either.'

Caleb was used to people objecting to the colour of his skin and for the most part it did not bother him at all. 'So, where does a man sleep?' he asked.

Both men laughed and nodded outside. 'See them two shacks opposite?' asked Royston. Caleb nodded. 'Them's bunkhouses. There's about forty bunks in each one...' Caleb must have shown his surprise. 'Most bunks are three high, one or two are two high and if you want a bed on its own you pays extra. Nobody here can afford the extra. They is twenty five cents a day a triple or a double and a single is ten cents a day extra. Food is extra. You gets the same thing twice a day, mornin' and evenin' an' it's the same every day—stew. Don't ask me what kind of stew but they do say that when a feller dies round here he don't get buried!' Both men laughed. 'Anyhow, Padre, what brings a man like you through here?'

'Pure chance,' said Caleb. 'I can assure you that nothing else would get me here.' That was not strictly true now that he had seen the likely potential in reward money. He resolved that shortly he was going to look through his collection of flyers and attempt to tie a few faces to pictures and rewards, starting with the men either side of him.

However, as interested in his fellow men as he might have been, it did not solve the immediate problem of just where he was going to sleep that night. He told his two self-appointed guardians that he intended an early start and was therefore going to retire early, bought them another drink each in the hope of securing some form of loyalty and possibly protection during the night and moved along the dirty counter to where the bartender—Peg-leg—was in the process of playing with a huge cockroach which he casually flicked away when he saw Caleb.

'What can I do for you, Reveren'?' asked Peg-leg. As he moved Caleb could see exactly why he was so named. His right leg appeared to be a single wooden peg, apparently from the knee downwards.

'Even a preacher needs to sleep somewhere,' said Caleb. 'But I have no special desire to share with my fellow humans, especially the present company. Do you have anywhere more private?'

Peg-leg gave a broad grin and looked about the room. 'Can't say as I blame you, I don't think even the fleas an' bedbugs fancy sleepin' with this lot.' He hunched across the counter confidentially. 'Two dollars buys you a night with one of my girls in your own room.'

'How about a room on my own without any company at all?' asked Caleb. 'All I want is a night's rest and an early start.'

'Ain't no problem with the early start,' grinned Peg-leg, 'I get up at dawn an' make sure everybody else does as well. Don't know about a room on your own though, most folk take one of the girls with 'em. My girls don't have regular rooms of their own so if you don't take one of 'em you'll be doin' her out of a bed too.'

Caleb felt in his pocket and pulled out a five dollar bill which he held tantalizingly in front of Peg-leg. 'This says I get a room of my own!' he suggested.

Peg-leg licked his lips and suddenly snatched the money and stuffed it into a pocket. 'I just remembered we do have a room spare tonight,' he said. He nodded to the rear of the room. 'Through that door over there, second on the right. Oh, an' if you want any breakfast that'll be ten cents extra.' Having heard what breakfast consisted of, Caleb indicated that he was prepared to forego that pleasure.

He was told that his horse was welcome to use one of the paddocks but he was advised that his saddle, harnesses and rifle would not be there in the morning if he did not take them with him to his room. He had already decided on just such a course of action before Peg-leg warned him.

The room was in keeping with the rest of the saloon in that it was rough and ready. He examined the palliasse with the expert eye of a man used to hunting for vermin and was rather surprised when it appeared reasonably free of livestock and even quite clean. There were two blankets and a pillow all of which seemed reasonably wholesome. Apart from removing his coat and his two gunbelts, Caleb remained fully dressed including his boots. His guns were removed from their holsters and placed beneath his pillow within easy reach. Light to the room consisted of one small candle stub, but it was enough for the night and for Caleb to study the sheaf of posters he had with him.

All the time he had been in the saloon he had been making careful notes of faces and even the odd name he overheard. It did not take him very long to turn up flyers of Royston Lockwood and Ben Staples. Royston Lockwood did appear to be the man's proper name, which was surprising since the vast majority resorted to other names in order to avoid detection, changing that when it became too well known.

Royston Lockwood was wanted for petty

robbery of three or four stores in three or four towns and the amount on offer for him—alive only—was the princely sum of fifty dollars. Caleb observed that fifty dollars was hardly worth the effort of taking the man to the nearest sheriff. Ben Staples—real name Ben Smith—was also only wanted for petty robberies and again only commanded a price of fifty dollars. Caleb smiled ruefully, both at the fact that Smith was a name most folk adopted and the fact that even $100 was not worth the effort unless he happened to be close to a sheriff.

However, there were at least two and probably three posters which interested him greatly. He was quite certain that the three had been in the saloon and was absolutely positive about two of them. The first was Clarence Porter, alias Charlie Jones, wanted in two states for murder and bank robbery, dead or alive with $2,000 dead and $2,500 alive. Caleb liked dead or alive posters and was always prepared to forego the extra if it was easier to deliver a dead body.

The second man was Mick (Slim) McCafferty, also know as Mick McConnel, wanted in three states for murder, rape, stage-coach robbery and bank robbery and he was on offer for $2,500 dead and $3,000 alive.

The third man, if he was correct, was Finbar O'Rourke, also wanted along with Mick McCafferty for the same murders, rape and robberies and he too laid claim to a very tempting $2,500 dead and $3,000 alive.

These three alone were more than sufficient reason for Caleb to want to hang about and eventually bring them or their dead bodies in front of a sheriff. In addition to these three he was quite certain that there were others on whom he had no information since it had been almost a month since he had last updated himself and that was two states ago. What he needed was to get to a proper town and replenish his stock of flyers, after handing over Clarence Porter, Mick McCafferty and Finbar O'Rourke. In addition to these three and possibly one or two others, he was quite certain that the remainder would also total up to quite an acceptable amount.

Sleep did not come too easily or quickly mainly due to the fact that the noise from the saloon seemed to go on until the early hours, but eventually it did and Caleb was surprised there was no trouble during the night.

Caleb was awake before dawn still un-decided as to what he should do. The obvious thing was to ride out and forget all about the outlaws and the money but as far as he was concerned life was never as simple as that and in any case he simply could not pass up the chance for such a big pay-day.

Daylight also revealed that the 'town' was much as he had seen it the previous night except that there were three other shacks standing back behind the saloon. One of these apparently housed Peg-leg, the owner of the saloon-cum-general store, and his woman. Still trying to decide on his next move, Caleb found himself idly wandering along the street to what looked like a rope bridge, which was just what it turned out to be.

The trail itself swung sharp right between two outcrops of jagged rock and then steeply, and very dangerous-looking, downwards. The rope bridge, wide enough to take a horse if one could be coaxed along it, spanned a deep chasm and as Caleb peered over the edge while he held on to a post anchoring one side of the bridge, he estimated that it was at least a 500 foot drop, possibly even more. A river forced its way through the chasm, swirling round and over jagged rocks. He mused that anyone unfortunate enough to fall stood no chance whatsoever.

The actual distance across the chasm was no more than 100 feet but it looked a very dangerous distance to him as the bridge was even now, in a very light wind, swaying alarmingly—at least it appeared alarming to him. He moved along and looked down the trail as it sloped and twisted downwards and then back at the bridge. It appeared that he had three choices of which way to go; back the way he had come; down the trail which presented its own hazards; or across the rope bridge. Of the three he was tempted to go back the way he had come since he was quite certain that he would never be able to coax his horse across the bridge even if it was fairly closely boarded.

A lone rider appeared from the saloon and showed Caleb how to get an unwilling horse across the bridge; He threw a piece of blanket across the horse's head, tied it on with a piece of thin rope and then led the horse on to the bridge. After a few paces the horse put up some resistance but after about five minutes had been coaxed to the other side. He later found out that this was the way almost everyone had to get their animals across. It appeared that pieces of blanket or sacking and lengths of thin rope were to be found at either end and it was an unwritten rule that each traveller left his piece of sacking at the other end for others to use.

As he walked back to the saloon, two half-dressed black figures appeared, each scratching vigorously at their bodies and occasionally removing some offending bedbug or tick. They saw Caleb and ambled towards him.

'See you had a room all to yourself,' grinned Ben almost enviously. 'Still, I suppose it's only right an' proper for a reveren' to have his own bed. You had breakfast?'

'I think I'll forego that pleasure,' said Caleb, feeling quite itchy himself at the sight of the two seeming to intensify their scratching.

'I think he means he ain't,' explained Royston.

'Can't say as I blame you,' said Ben. 'It's just what wasn't eaten yesterday.'

'Maybe you can tell me,' said Caleb. 'Where's the nearest town or city?'

The two looked at each other slightly puzzled for a moment. 'Don't know if you'd call it a city or not, but there's Rose Creek about twenty miles over the bridge.'

'Does it have a sheriff?' asked Caleb.

'Sure does,' grunted Royston. 'We ought to know, he made pretty damned sure we left town in double-quick time. It seems the only thing he had against us was the colour of our skin. Mind, we've been run out of better places than that before now!' They both laughed.

'What you want a sheriff for anyhow?' asked Ben.

'I just like to know,' said Caleb. 'How long are you boys staying in this hell-hole?'

Again they looked questioningly at each other and shrugged. 'Ain't even thought about it,' said Royston. 'We've been here three days, I guess it's about time we was movin' on.'

'What about some of the others,' said Caleb, 'do you know how long somebody like Porter, McCafferty and O'Rourke are likely to hang around?'

'How the hell did you know their names?' demanded Ben suspiciously.

'I know a lot of things,' smiled Caleb. 'I make it my business to know as much as possible about anyone I meet. For instance I know that you two are Royston Lockwood and Ben Staples because you have already told me and I know that you are wanted in various places for some rather petty robberies.'

Ben's hand gripped the rather old Adams at his side and he stared challengingly at Caleb who simply returned the stare and casually flicked aside one edge of his long coat to reveal a modern Colt. For a moment Ben appeared uneasy as he licked his lips and his hand slowly loosened its grip on his Adams.

'OK, so you know who we are and what we've done,' said Ben. 'I don't know why a preacher should want to know things like that but I'll let it pass.'

Caleb nodded. 'I was asking about Porter, McCafferty and O'Rourke.'

'Another three or four days at least,' said Royston looking at the preacher in a new light. 'I heard one of 'em talkin' this mornin'. They're waitin' for somethin' to go quiet before they move. What you askin' for?'

Caleb grinned but refused to enlighten them. 'How would you like to stay on here for a few days more—at my expense? I'll pay for your beds and food and I'll even give you five dollars for your drink.'

The two looked at each other and then at Caleb. 'Who we got to kill?'

'Who said anything about killing anyone?' asked Caleb. 'All I want you to do is stay here and keep an eye on Porter, McCafferty and O'Rourke. If you can find out anything of their plans I'll even pay you more.'

'Are you sure you're a preacher?' asked Royston, suspiciously.

'Fully ordained!' grinned Caleb.

TWO

Caleb took his horse to the rope bridge, tied a piece of sacking round its head and led it on to the slightly swaying boards. After a few feet the horse refused to go any further and he spent a few agonizing minutes trying to coax her forward. Slowly but surely he managed to lead her across and he was probably more relieved than she was when they finally clambered on to solid ground on the other side.

Royston and Ben had agreed to stay, but for no more than four days. If he had not returned in that time it was agreed that they could do whatever they wanted. They had been very curious as to what he was up to but he had not enlightened them knowing that if they did know they would probably not co-operate.

Once across the chasm the trail descended quite steeply at first, but not as steeply as it had appeared to do on the other side and after about a mile of twisting and turning it gradually became easier, still descending and eventually ran through thick forest for about another three miles.

A fork in the trail proclaimed Rose Creek to the right as still being twenty miles. There was no destination indicated on the other trail which he knew probably meant that it was a lot further to wherever it did lead to. Although flat and easy going, the twenty miles seemed more like thirty but eventually Caleb could see evidence of a town.

Rose Creek was larger than he had expected, consisting of two main streets, several stores of various kinds, two saloons, a bank and the sheriff's office next door to each other being the only two brickbuilt buildings in town.

His arrival attracted a certain amount of idle curiosity and he was uncertain if this was because he was dressed in the garb of a preacher or because he was black. He rather suspected that it was the latter.

He pulled up outside the sheriff's office where a tall, thin man eyed him suspiciously from the comfort of a chair raked back against the wall. A badge on the man's chest indicated that this was the sheriff himself. There was even more suspicion when Caleb mounted the boardwalk and stood over him.

'Yeh?' grunted the sheriff as he allowed his chair to gain its natural upright position. 'You got a problem?'

'Not particularly,' grinned Caleb. 'Allow me to introduce myself. Caleb Black, the

Reverend Caleb Black, Black by name and black by colour.'

'Pleased to meet you, Reverend,' replied the sheriff not very convincingly.

Caleb deliberately and rather exaggeratedly looked about. 'Nice town you have here.'

'It's all right I suppose,' grunted the sheriff. 'It suits most folk who live here. What can I do for you, Reverend?'

Caleb pulled up another chair, smiled and sat alongside him, obviously to the sheriff's discomfort. 'I have just come through the mountains, from some place which doesn't appear to have any name, there's a rope bridge across a chasm...'

'Everybody knows where that is,' grunted the sheriff. 'Anyone who's got any sense don't ever go anywhere near there, you're more likely to end up dead for the change in your pocket. I would have thought that was just about the last place a man of the church would go.'

'On the contrary,' grinned Caleb. 'It's just the sort of place a man of the cloth should go. There are more souls to be saved in a place like that than most other places.'

The sheriff gave a derisive laugh. 'I guess you're right there, Reverend, but I don't give much for your chances of success.'

This time Caleb laughed. 'Neither do I. Obviously the type of inhabitants are well known to you. That brings me to the real reason for my being here now. Do you know exactly who is up there?'

The sheriff studied Caleb for a few moments and he did not miss at least one gun strapped to the preacher's thigh. 'Are you really a preacher?' he asked.

Caleb smiled and patted the gun in view, the other still hidden by his coat. 'The Lord moves in mysterious ways, Sheriff,' he said. 'I am indeed an ordained preacher and I have here letters to prove it...' He pulled some papers out of his inside pocket and handed them to the sheriff who scanned them briefly and handed them back. 'In my other life I am a bounty hunter.' If the sheriff was surprised he certainly did not show it. 'I know most people find the two don't go together,' continued Caleb, 'but even a man of the cloth needs to earn a living, especially when he doesn't have a regular parish.'

'Each to his own I suppose,' grunted the sheriff. 'So how does this affect me?'

'There's a lot of reward money sitting up there,' said Caleb, 'reward money I would very much like to get my hands on.'

The sheriff laughed derisively again and hunched forward slightly. 'Reverend, there's been at least four other bounty hunters through here in the last month and each one has said more-or-less the same thing. I know exactly what you are goin' to say: you want to know if you can collect if you bring 'em here. Sure, that's no problem. The only problem you've got is actually bringin' 'em here, dead or alive. The last bounty hunter left town just over a week ago sayin' he would be back in three days; so far I haven't seen hair nor hide of him nor any of the others.'

'If you know these outlaws are up there, why don't you get up there and bring a few in yourself?' asked Caleb.

'That's simple,' laughed the sheriff, 'I like livin'!'

'You could form a posse,' suggested Caleb.

Once again the sheriff laughed derisively. 'Reverend, you've been up there, you've seen the place an' where it is. They could hold out for years. Besides, I did think about it once and even tried to get some folk together but they're all like me, they is too fond of livin'. Anyhow, they don't bother us down here so why the hell should we go lookin' for trouble?'

'For a lot of reward money,' said Caleb.

'Dead men don't need money!' said the sheriff. 'Anyhow, it'd be doin' folk like you out of business. If you think you can succeed where everyone else has failed, be my guest, I'll be more than happy to arrange for the reward to be paid. There was even a marshal and two deputies tried it about a year ago. They disappeared too.'

'OK,' said Caleb, 'I'll go along with what you say and I think I can bring a few of them in. What I want from you, apart from knowing that you can arrange for the payment of the reward, is an update on any posters you may have.'

'No problem at all,' nodded the sheriff. 'I can't see that it'll do any good though. Even if you do bring some of 'em in, they're just like rats. As soon as one moves out another moves in. OK, I'll give you what I've got, come on inside.' He stood up and led Caleb into the office where he pulled some posters from a drawer and dropped them on the desk. 'Help yourself,' he said. 'There's no guarantee just who is up there and who isn't.'

Caleb picked up the posters and slowly looked through them and selected some he knew he did not have. He dropped the posters relating to Porter, McCafferty and O'Rourke on the desk.

'These three are there for a start,' he said. 'There's one or two others here who look familiar but I can't be certain.'

The sheriff picked up the three posters and grunted. 'They're well off their territory; are you sure it's them?'

'Positive!' asserted Caleb. 'I never forget

faces; my living depends on it.'

'I sometimes think this job is dangerous enough,' nodded the sheriff, 'but I think you've chosen an even more dangerous one. If I were you I'd stick to preachin'.'

Caleb smiled and folded the posters and put them in his pocket. 'I may be a preacher, Sheriff, but I have found that there are not too many places where people are prepared to take on a black preacher full time.'

'We ain't got no preacher in Rose Creek at the moment,' said the sheriff. 'It could be that you could set up here.'

Caleb smiled knowingly. 'And how long do you think I'd last? As soon as I rode into town I knew exactly what the feeling towards black folk was. It took you all your time to even talk to me.'

The sheriff smiled and nodded. 'I guess that's the way most folk are round here. Even so, there's quite a few folk who would welcome a preacher right now. I know of two couples who want to get married and at least three christenin's. I reckon you could be usefully employed for at least a week no matter what your colour.'

'Is that an offer?' grinned Caleb.

'It is as far as I'm concerned,' replied the sheriff. 'If you want to take it up I'll ask around.'

'Is there a church?'

The sheriff nodded in the direction of the other street which crossed just below his office. 'Down by the livery stable,' he said. 'Last time it was used proper was about two years ago. We had a preacher for a good many years but he died and there ain't been nobody since.'

'So how do people cope with things like weddings and funerals?' asked Caleb.

'The last time anyone got married they had to go to Byron, that's about two days' ride. Most just don't bother an' move in together.'

Caleb thought about it for a few moments and then nodded. 'OK, if that's what folk want I'll do it but I don't think I'll stay too long. I guess I wasn't being strictly honest when I said I couldn't get a regular parish, the truth is that I'm a wanderer by nature.'

The sheriff glanced at Caleb's gun and nodded. 'Can you use that thing?' he asked. 'It still don't sit right with me seein' a preacher wearin' a gun and earnin' his livin' by bounty huntin'.' Caleb grinned and pulled back both sides of his coat to reveal a gun on his other thigh. The sheriff seemed very impressed and nodded sagely. 'I've only ever seen one other man wearin' two guns,' he continued, 'and he could use both. Lookin' at you an' the way you wear those things I'd say you knew how to use both as well.'

'As a good many have discovered to their cost,' said Caleb. 'And before you ask, I do not find it difficult to shoot a man and reconcile it with my beliefs. I was brought up to believe in an eye for an eye.'

'It had crossed my mind,' said the sheriff. 'Still, that's none of my business. So what is your plan now? I reckon that if folk want to use you as a preacher they ought to do it before you go off on this wild scheme of bringin' in outlaws from up at No-Name.' He laughed to himself. 'Strange that, the place never has had a name but then again it has always been known as No-Name. Everybody knows exactly where you're talkin' about when you say "No-Name". Anyway, I don't doubt that you are very good with them guns but that could be said of others and they've all failed.'

'They haven't all been preachers!' said Caleb. 'I can't afford to miss this chance. I have no idea just how long they are staying up there or which way they intend going, although I do have a couple of pairs of ears and eyes watching over them.'

'Royston Lockwood and Ben Staples?' said the sheriff.

'You remember them!' observed Caleb. 'You've got a couple of posters out on them too. Why didn't you arrest them when they came through? They told me you couldn't get them out of town fast enough.'

'Small beer!' said the sheriff. 'At fifty dollars apiece they just weren't worth the bother. It would've cost more'n that to keep 'em and transport 'em to prison.'

'Well hopefully they're working for me

at this moment,' said Caleb. 'Mind you, I wouldn't trust either of them but a little money can work wonders.'

'Do they know you're a bounty hunter?' asked the sheriff.

'I haven't told them and I don't really think either of them is bright enough to work it out,' smiled Caleb. 'Well, thanks for your time, Sheriff, right now I'm hungry, is there anywhere I can get a big steak? I've been dreaming about an enormous steak for almost two weeks now.'

'No problem,' grinned the sheriff. 'The best place is Alma's Eatin' House, she serves the biggest and best steaks you'll ever find. It ain't nothin' special, just a kitchen with benches and tables outside under canvas. The biggest trouble is the flies, but then you won't get away from them even in the hotel. The hotel is fine for the ladies who like fancy afternoon teas but Alma looks after the appetites of the miners.'

'Miners?' queried Caleb.

'Sure, there's two big mines, one either

side of the river, owned by some big companies from back East. That's the main reason Rose Creek is here, most folk work for one or other of the mines in one way or another.'

'Alma's Eatin' House sounds just about perfect,' said Caleb. 'She doesn't mind feeding black men does she?'

'As long as your money's the same colour as anyone else's, she couldn't care less,' said the sheriff.

Caleb followed the sheriff's directions and soon found Alma's Eatin' House which did indeed turn out to be a wooden shack surrounded on three sides by a roof of canvas and open sided. There were already about ten men eating and apart from a brief cursory glance at Caleb as he entered and found himself a seat, their interest was obviously in their steaks.

The sheriff had been right about the flies, although even out in the desert when there appeared to be no possibility of any form of life, Caleb had found out that flies and ticks miraculously appeared from nowhere. A large, rather untidy woman bustled out of the kitchen, looked at Caleb questioningly and waited.

'The largest steak you have,' he said.

'Steaks is all you get here,' she sniffed and wiped her nose on her not-so-clean apron. 'There's three sizes, small, medium an' large. Small is about so big...' She indicated a size with her hands and a thickness of about an inch. 'Medium is about so big...' She repeated the operation. 'And large is about this size an' about one and half inches thick. If you want bigger I guess I can make it thicker.'

Actually the size she had indicated as small appeared large to Caleb and the large seemed far too much but he had been looking forward to a big steak and he opted for the large. It took about ten minutes for the meal to arrive and, as well as the most enormous steak he had ever seen, there were also liberal portions of potatoes, turnips and turnip greens.

The steak was tender and very tasty and it took him all his time to eat it, but he surprised himself and managed to finish it and even most of the vegetables.

Much to his surprise a large mug of coffee was suddenly placed in front of him and Alma enquired as to whether he wanted some apple pie or not. Caleb tried to hold back a belch but failed and apologized. The apology seemed to surprise her more than the belch. He thought about it for a moment and decided—very reluctantly since he had not eaten apple pie for a long time—that he simply could not force another morsel of food down his throat. The one thing he was now certain of was that at the next opportunity he would visit Alma's Eatin' House again but the next time he would order a smaller steak and the apple pie. He paid the one dollar asked for and considered it money very well spent.

The effect of a good meal and the heat of the afternoon decided Caleb that a couple of hours sleeping things off would be a very good idea and he took his horse down by the river where he found a clump of trees for shade, good grass for his horse and plenty of water should either of them need it. He unsaddled his horse and used the saddle as a pillow and very quickly was sound asleep.

He woke up with a start and automatically snatched his gun as he looked up into a face hovering above him. The face came into focus as belonging to the sheriff. He smiled and lowered the gun.

'You shouldn't creep up on folk like that,' he said. 'I might have shot you.'

'And you could've been dead too,' said the sheriff. 'I was standin' over you for two or three minutes.'

Caleb smiled and nodded. 'Probably I could have been,' he conceded. 'I have discovered though that if someone is asleep it is very rare for anyone to simply shoot them, it seems that the killer has to wake his victim first. I don't quite understand why, but that's the way it seems to me, at least with a man. I did come across a woman who shot her man while he was asleep because she knew she could never do it if he looked at her.'

'I wouldn't know about things like that,' said the sheriff. 'I just thought I ought to tell you that four men have just come into town, all with a thousand dollars dead or alive on their heads.'

'So why haven't you tackled them?' asked Caleb.

'I said there were four of 'em,' replied the sheriff, 'and I know they're all good gunmen and I'm too fond of livin'.'

'So you want me to take care of them?' grinned Caleb sitting up and stretching.

'What you do is entirely up to you,' said the sheriff. 'I'm goin' to do nothin'. You claim to make your livin' bounty huntin', I just thought I'd let you know a pay day just rode in.'

'Where are they?' asked Caleb.

'In the saloon at the moment but I heard 'em askin' about somewhere to eat an' they were directed to Alma's.'

'Names?' asked Caleb. The sheriff produced four posters, four which Caleb had taken copies of simply because he did not have them. He had not expected to find the men in No-Name.

Caleb looked through the posters and nodded approvingly. 'Carl Smith, Pedro

Sanchez, Luke Gray and Amos Taylor. I've heard of them. It seems as though all the outlaws are gathering but it is probably just chance. OK, I'll see what I can do. Thanks for the information.'

'I'll tell Jake Mansell to get your coffin ready!' grinned the sheriff.

Caleb ignored the remark and adjusted his twin gun belts, checked both guns were fully loaded and decided that his horse and saddle would be safe enough where they were, although he did ask the sheriff to take command of his rifle.

'I prefer hand guns,' explained Caleb, 'and I certainly can't use both if I have a rifle as well. Dead or alive you say? How do you want them?'

'Dead would sure save a whole lot of trouble,' said the sheriff. 'Mind, I reckon it's you who'll end up dead and if you do I shan't do anythin' about it 'cos I know it was you who set out to kill them.'

'I thank you for your confidence!' grinned Caleb as he climbed up the river bank and headed in the direction of the saloon. He was just in time to see the four men disappearing round a corner heading in the direction of Alma's Eatin' House and he followed them.

There were five other customers spread around as the four outlaws seated themselves but as soon as Caleb went up to them and dropped the Wanted posters in front of them, there was suddenly only the four outlaws and Caleb, although the steaks the other five had been eating also disappeared along with the men.

Four snarling faces sneered up at Caleb and four hands went for four guns. The benches clattered backwards and four shots rang out...

'If I hadn't seen it with my own eyes I'd never have believed it,' said the sheriff with obvious admiration in his voice and eyes. 'You must've been pretty damned sure of yourself.'

'I had surprise on my side,' said Caleb as he watched the four bodies being loaded on to Jake Mansell's wagon. 'They were also sitting down and no man can draw fast when he's sitting. That's four thousand dollars you owe me, Sheriff. How long do I have to wait?'

'It'll take about two days,' said the sheriff. 'I can authorize up to one hundred dollars but anythin' over that I have to send a wire to Phoenix and get clearance.'

'I guess I can wait,' smiled Caleb.

'It could be that you won't be able to collect, not if you are still goin' after them three out at No-Name,' said the sheriff.

'And it could be that you'll be sending another wire,' smiled Caleb.

By that time almost the entire population of Rose Creek had gathered to stand and stare at the strange, black preacher who had just killed four outlaws. Word had spread very quickly both of the killings and the fact that Caleb was a preacher and as the bodies were taken away two elderly ladies cautiously approached Caleb.

'Is it true that you are a priest?' asked the thinner of the two ladies.

'I guess so,' admitted Caleb. 'I don't like the word "priest", though I am a fully ordained preacher. I always think of priests being Catholic, which I am not.'

The woman appeared to be quite relieved that Caleb was not a Catholic but it was plain that she was not too sure about the colour of his skin. She looked at her companion and they both nodded.

'Are you able to administer the sacraments?' she asked.

'Naturally,' said Caleb. He produced the papers which confirmed his position and offered them to the ladies. They glanced through them and appeared satisfied. 'How can I help you, ladies?'

'Well, having just witnessed four bodies being taken away,' said the stouter woman, 'I am not really so sure that you can. We don't doubt that you are a preacher but in our eyes it is not normal for priests of any kind to go around killing people, not even vicious outlaws. The word is that you are also a bounty hunter, is that true?'

'Even a man of the cloth must eat,' said Caleb. 'As to me being a bounty hunter it is true, but I feel I am doing God's work in bringing sinners to justice or to answer to the Lord for what they have done. I am merely an instrument of the Lord.'

The two ladies looked at each other again and once again nodded. 'It still doesn't seem right,' said the thinner woman.

'The Lord works in mysterious ways,' smiled Caleb.

'Indeed He does!' sighed the stout woman. 'Very well, we must accept the facts as they are...'

'Including the colour of my skin?' said Caleb.

The stout woman blushed and shuffled uneasily. 'That is something that you cannot do anything about,' she said. 'It does not matter as far as we are concerned.'

The thinner woman was slightly more honest. 'I used to own slaves,' she said proudly, 'and I must confess that I would much prefer it if you were white, but like my friend I must accept the status quo. Slavery is a thing of the past and I must accept it but that does not mean that I must like it. Now, to business. This town is in urgent need of the services of a priest or preacher and at least you have the advantage that you are not Catholic...'

'Ladies,' grinned Caleb. 'I do have some other business to attend which will take me away for a few days but when I return I shall be only too happy to perform whatever service I am able.'

'I fail to see what other business that can be,' snorted the thin woman. 'However, if that's the way it must be then so be it.'

'Four days at the outside,' said Caleb. 'That's a promise!'

THREE

Caleb arrived back in No-Name just before dusk and nobody seemed more surprised to see him than Royston and Ben, although the owner of the saloon-cum-store was almost as amazed but if any of the others were surprised, they certainly did not show it other than mild expressions of curiosity. Porter, McCafferty and O'Rourke gave him a brief glance and made some comment he did not hear and continued with the game of cards in which they were engrossed.

'We thought we'd seen the last of you,' observed Royston. 'And we sure didn't expect you back today.'

'I sorted out my business in Rose Creek sooner than I expected,' said Caleb. 'Have you found anything out?'

'Not a thing,' said Ben. 'All they've done is sit here playin' cards all day. Glad you came back though, we've only got two dollars left.'

'You've drunk that lot already!' exclaimed Caleb.

'Some of it,' grinned Royston, 'Ben here fancied one of the girls, that took care of most of it. We got to talkin' while you was away, wonderin' just why you was so interested in them three...' He nodded across the room at the card players. 'Why should a preacher be so interested in the likes of them, we asked ourselves? The other thing we asked was why should a preacher be wearin' a gun? We ain't too bright, neither of us can read or write, but then neither can most black men. You though, you're different. If you're a preacher you must be able to read an' write which makes you somethin' different.'

'And what conclusion did you arrive at?' smiled Caleb as he ordered beers.

'There you go again,' grumbled Ben, 'usin' fancy words just like I heard white folks do on the plantation when I was a kid.'

'You were a slave?' asked Caleb.

'Well, we was both born on plantations an' our folks was all slaves, so I guess that means we was slaves too.'

'My parents were runaway slaves too,' said Caleb, 'but I was born up north. I'm sorry if I use words you can't understand, I can't help it. I guess that's what education does for you. What I meant was, after you had asked yourselves those questions, what did you decide?'

'We decided that those men must have done somethin' to you or your family and you is out for revenge,' said Royston.

'Something like that,' agreed Ben.

'So why don't you just walk up to 'em and kill 'em?' asked Ben. 'Nobody here would bother an' there sure ain't no law to worry about it.'

Caleb sighed and shook his head. 'I wish things were as easy as that,' he said. 'The fact that I am a man of the cloth prevents me from simply murdering people no matter who they are and what they've done.' That was not true but he thought it a good enough explanation for the moment.

Royston and Ben thought about that for a moment and eventually nodded their understanding. 'Yeh,' said Ben. 'I guess it does make it kinda difficult. OK, so what do you want us to do?'

'An' don't say we are to kill 'em,' said Royston. 'I know we're wanted for some petty thievin' an' such like, but as yet we ain't wanted for murder an' that's the way we intend to keep it.'

'Very wise,' smiled Caleb. 'I haven't given it a lot of thought, I'll have to let you know, but I have the feeling that I shall need you to be around for some time yet.'

'We ain't got nothin' else to do,' said

Ben. 'You just keep us supplied with a few dollars an' we'll be here when you need us. Anyhow, what did you go into Rose Creek for?'

'I went to tell the sheriff that those three were here,' said Caleb. That at least was true. 'I wanted him to get up a posse and arrest them.'

They both laughed. 'And he told you he wasn't interested!' said Ben. 'We could've told you that; in fact I think we did warn you that he didn't like blacks in his town.'

'That you did,' agreed Caleb. 'You were right as well, although he didn't try to run me out.'

'That's 'cos you is a preacher an' you got book learnin',' said Royston. 'I knew a man like you once, long time ago when we was still on the plantation. He just rode into town an' started to preach to us. The white bosses didn't like it but because he warn't no slave they didn't do nothin'. Mind, they did make life pretty uncomfortable for him an' he rode out after three months, but at least he was free to ride out, we weren't.'

'But you are now,' said Caleb.

They both shrugged. 'That's about all,' said Ben. 'Most folk where we come from is still tied to the plantations. We was supposed to get our freedom but the only thing was nobody ain't got no place to be free to go. In some ways my folks was better off as slaves, at least they got their house an' food for nothin'. After we was freed the white bosses started chargin' us rents an' we had to buy our food an' they sure didn't pay much wages. In fact most didn't pay proper money, they gave what they called tokens which could only be spent in the white man's stores, so we was still slaves really.'

'We are all slaves really,' said Caleb. 'Anyhow, you just hang around for a while. I see you both wear guns, can you use them?'

They glanced at each other briefly. 'I guess we can if we have to. It ain't often we have to; we can't afford it, bullets cost money which we don't have.'

'Then let's hope you don't have to,'

said Caleb. 'Right now I need to organize somewhere to sleep.' He called the owner of the saloon and arranged for the same room he had occupied the previous night, although it cost him another five dollars. After once again bringing his saddle and rifle into the room, he returned to the bar where the three men were still playing cards. On an impulse he walked over to them and for a couple of minutes he stood and watched.

Finbar O'Rourke eventually looked up and stared at Caleb for some time before speaking. 'Can we do somethin' for you?' he asked.

'It's a long time since I played poker,' said Caleb. 'Mind if I sit in?'

The three men looked at each other and finally nodded, each shuffling his chair round slightly while Caleb brought up a fourth and Mick McCafferty dealt out four hands. Caleb picked up his cards and saw that he had two kings. He changed three cards and now found himself with two kings and two threes. He had never been a regular poker player but he knew enough to know that two pairs was a good hand.

They were only playing for pennies and Caleb emptied a handful of change on to the table and made his bid of ten cents. It appeared that even this was too much for Clarence Porter and O'Rourke as they folded immediately. McCafferty studied his cards for a few moments and then looked at the preacher and pushed forward his ten cents and another ten cents.

'I think you're bluffin'!' he said.

'I wouldn't know how to,' smiled Caleb. 'What do I do now? It's been a long time since I even had any cards in my hand.'

The three men glanced at each other knowingly before O'Rourke told him that if he wanted to continue it would cost him another twenty cents plus an increase in stake. This continued twice more until McCafferty had only enough money left to call Caleb's hand. Caleb spread his two pairs on the table and McCafferty snorted in disgust and threw his cards on the table.

'I take it that means I've won,' said Caleb reaching out and scooping the money towards him.

'Beginner's luck!' snarled McCafferty.

'Perhaps the Lord is on my side,' grinned Caleb. 'Fancy another hand?'

The three grunted and McCafferty fumbled in his pocket and found some more change. The cards were dealt again and Caleb found himself with a pair of nines. He changed three cards and still had a pair of nines. This time McCafferty and Porter folded and once again, after a few raised stakes, Caleb found himself scooping the pot against O'Rourke's pair of sevens.

'You sure it's been a long time since you played?' asked O'Rourke.

'Positive,' grinned Caleb.

'Anyhow,' continued O'Rourke, 'what the hell brings a man like you here? You ain't wanted by the law, I'll gamble on that any time. When you rode out this mornin' we thought that was the last we'd seen of you. What the hell brought you back here? It wasn't the food or the company that's for sure.'

'I'm a preacher, remember,' said Caleb. 'My job is to convert lost souls and as far as I can see there's nobody more lost than all the folk here right now.'

'Too right about that!' laughed McCafferty. 'I don't give you much chance of convertin' nobody here though, we is all too far gone.'

'Nobody is too far gone,' said Caleb. 'We all have a value, even you.' All three stared at Caleb hard and eventually O'Rourke broke the silence.

'What exactly does that mean?' he growled.

'It means exactly what I say,' replied Caleb. 'It's obvious that you are men who are accustomed to violence, even that you have killed other men, but that does not mean that your souls are worthless. Somewhere deep inside you, inside all of us, there is some good.'

'Fancy words, Preacher,' sneered McCafferty. 'If there is a Heaven or a Hell or a God, it's somethin' that ain't no use to us in this life. The reality is that all three of us are worth somethin', but only as far as the law is concerned.'

'Is that why you are here?' asked Caleb

pretending he knew nothing. 'Hiding from the law in a place like this doesn't seem much of a life to me.'

'It ain't,' admitted McCafferty, 'but at the moment it's the only choice we've got.'

'And do you think you are safe here?' prodded Caleb. 'Do you think the law does not know where you are and might come looking for you?'

'Reveren'!' sighed O'Rourke. 'It seems to me that you are askin' too many damn fool questions. I don't buy that bit about you comin' back here to save our souls. I reckon you went into Rose Creek, discovered just how much we was worth to the law and came back to try your luck.'

Caleb laughed. 'Become what I believe they call a bounty hunter you mean?' he said. 'How long do you think I would last in a place like this if that was my idea? There are about twenty men here and I have no doubt that all of them are wanted by the law for something or other and that alone must make it a bounty-hunter's paradise, but do you really believe that any such person would stand a chance? For instance, I would probably have to kill everyone to guarantee staying alive and I can't really see me or anyone else achieving that. After that I would have the problem of getting all those bodies back to where I could claim any reward money. No, my friends, the pure practicalities far outweigh any possible financial attraction the rewards out on you may have to offer.'

'What's he sayin'?' asked Clarence Porter.

'I think he's tellin' us he ain't no bounty hunter,' grinned Finbar O'Rourke. 'That is what you're tryin' to say ain't it, Reverend?'

'I believe that's what I just said,' smiled Caleb.

'Then just say so,' grumbled Porter. 'Don't go usin' all them fancy words. That's the trouble with all you preachers, you use a lot of words just to say nothin'.'

Caleb laughed and picked up the pack of cards and shuffled them, finding it quite difficult due to their well-worn condition. 'My two black friends over there...' He nodded at Royston and Ben who were propping up the counter each supping a beer. 'They have also complained I use too many big words. The trouble is I don't know too many short ones that people like you can understand. Now, who wants another game?'

The three men grunted and seemed resigned to the fact that they were never going to fully understand Caleb and agreed to another game. This time Caleb ensured that he lost a few hands even though he was dealt some very good ones. At the end of the session he had lost just over one dollar which appeared to have been equally divided between the three of them and honour seemed satisfied. Eventually all four decided it was time for some sleep.

Caleb was not at all certain if he had heard a noise or not, all he knew was that he was now suddenly fully awake and fully alert. His room had only one small window and since it appeared totally dark outside, it was not much use in highlighting anything. However, he had the very distinct feeling that he was not alone. His hand had already grasped one of his guns under his pillow but apart from that, as far as he knew, he had not moved a muscle. His ears strained and this time he quite definitely heard a board creak close by and a slight intake of breath but he still waited.

His bed was up against the right-hand wall and he was lying with his face towards the other wall and the door. He knew he had locked the door but at the same time he knew that even a small child could very quickly and easily unlock it but he had not heard the door open or close and in the very dim light he was certain that it was now closed.

Suddenly he was aware of something very dark alongside his bed and reaching down to his saddlebags. 'Lost something!?' rasped Caleb, the gun in his hand pointing at the shape. The figure suddenly loomed upwards and Caleb was aware of a dull thud into his shoulder. The gun in his hand roared into life and delivered death; the figure gasped briefly and thudded to the floor. Immediately Caleb was on his feet and striking a match to light the small candle on the table at his bedside. At the same time there were the unmistakable sounds of feet pounding along the small corridor followed by a hammering on his door.

'You all right, Reverend?' came the voice of Peg-leg. 'What was that shootin'?'

'I'm all right,' called Caleb. 'It seems I have had a visitor. Come on in.'

The door opened and two people stood there, one of them holding an oil lamp. Peg-leg hobbled into the room and stared down at the lifeless figure on the floor and then at Caleb.

'That's Sam Jones,' said the woman with Peg-leg. 'What's he doin' here?'

'At the present moment he is not doing a thing,' said Caleb. 'All I know is I am bleeding quite badly, I think he stabbed me.'

The lamp was lifted and the woman looked at Caleb's shoulder and grunted her agreement that he had been stabbed. 'I ain't no doctor,' she said, 'but I'll see what I can do. I've dealt with worse before now.

'He's dead,' announced Peg-leg after turning the body over. 'Stupid bastard. I know he was broke and he had made some comment about you seemin' to have plenty.'

'Well he won't need any money now,' observed Caleb.

By that time almost everyone from the bunkhouses had crammed into the corridor all demanding to know what had happened, including a man whom Peg-leg later identified to Caleb as Sam Jones's constant companion, Whispering Thomas, so named because he had a throat injury which meant that he could only talk in whispers and at times not at all.

The body was removed from Caleb's room and unceremoniously dumped in one of the empty buildings to await burial in the morning. However, when morning came and someone went to look at the body, it was discovered that it was completely naked and all Jones's belongings had somehow vanished into thin air.

In the meantime Caleb was taken back to the shack where Peg-leg and his woman slept and she made a passable job of cleaning up the wound in Caleb's shoulder remarking that God must have been watching over him since had the knife entered about three inches lower he would certainly have been dead. Caleb agreed with her and politely refused her offer to stitch the wound, a task which she assured him, she had performed many times with great success. Caleb returned to his room to discover Royston and Ben in residence but they did not appear to have looked through his belongings.

'Just thought we'd better keep an eye on your things,' said Royston. 'Most likely there would've been nothin' left by the time you came back if we hadn't.'

'I thank you for your concern,' said Caleb. 'I appreciate it. I'll be OK now, you can go back to bed.'

'If you're sure,' said Ben. 'We can stay

if you want, we don't mind sleepin' on the floor.'

Caleb assured them that he would be perfectly all right, he certainly did not relish the idea of spending the remainder of the night in the same room and they somewhat reluctantly left. However, Royston did warn him that Whispering Thomas had sworn vengeance for the death of his friend.

The burial of Sam Jones was a very matter-of-fact affair, Whispering Thomas refusing to allow Caleb to conduct any form of service which, on reflection, Caleb had to admit would have appeared rather inappropriate since it was he who had killed the man. Earlier, Caleb had looked through his Wanted posters and found two relating to both Sam Jones and Whispering Thomas and both offering $100 alive. Neither was known as a killer and Caleb thought that Whispering's threats were little more than just threats, although he was ready to believe that he just might carry them out, especially in No-Name with little chance of being hunted for them.

All the other temporary residents of No-Name seemed to have forgotten the incident almost as soon as they had woken up and the only witnesses to the burial of Sam Jones were Peg-leg, Caleb, Whispering Thomas and Royston Lockwood. It appeared that Ben Staples had something of an aversion to seeing people buried. The crude cemetery itself was nothing more than a patch of soft ground between rocky outcrops and already contained about ten other obvious graves and about five other sites which could have been. There was no attempt at providing a coffin, the naked body, having been stripped during the night, simply thrown into the hole. It was shortly after the internment of Sam Jones, as Caleb attended to his horse in the paddock opposite the saloon, that Whispering Thomas acted...

The first Caleb knew of anything was when a voice, which turned out to be

Royston, suddenly yelled out. Instinct more than anything made Caleb react in the manner he had become used to in such circumstances.

He drew one gun, leaving the other covered by his long coat as was his usual habit, dropped to one knee and gave a very quick look around, all of which happened in about two seconds, saw a figure a few yards away apparently aiming a gun at him and he fired.

There were two shots; the first smashed into the wooden fence post close to Caleb's head and the other struck its target with deadly accuracy as he saw the figure clutch briefly at his chest and then slump headlong on to the ground. Caleb slowly rose to his feet and looked warily around. The sound of a slow handclap came from just behind him and he turned to see Finbar O'Rourke and Mick McCafferty lounging on the hitching rail outside the saloon.

'Very fancy!' said Finbar O'Rourke giving another few claps. 'Now I know you ain't just some ordinary preacher. I've seen some pretty fast reactions in my time but I reckon that was just about the fastest draw I ever did see.'

'I never said I didn't know how to use a gun,' said Caleb replacing it in its holster. At the same time he took care to ensure that his second gun remained hidden. More than once his life had depended upon the fact that he wore two guns and was able to use either hand and that people had always assumed that he only had the one. Thus far it appeared that nobody had noticed this fact and that was just how he wanted things to stay.

Peg-leg appeared in the doorway and glanced at the body before making some remark about someone else having to dig the damned hole since he was too busy. Caleb volunteered Royston and Ben for the job but had to promise them five dollars. An hour later Whispering Thomas was thrown into a hole alongside his friend, this time fully clothed but it was noticeable that his gun and belt were missing and his pockets empty. The death of the two men meant that there were now two saddles spare of which Peg-leg immediately took possession and placed in his store as being for sale. Caleb did notice that some secondhand clothing and another old Adams pistol and a gun belt now on sale looked very familiar but he made no comment.

The first incident had been passed off by everyone as just one of those things that can happen in the night but the second had those same people looking at the preacher in a very new light and certainly with a great deal more respect. In fact six of them decided that it was time to be on their way and rode off southwards, the direction from which Caleb had come. Caleb was not too worried by the departure of these men since he had no flyers on two of them and therefore were probably not too important and of the remaining four only one had more than $50 on his head and that was only $100. His main quarry, Clarence Porter, Mick McCafferty and Finbar O'Rourke seemed firmly entrenched.

All this had happened well before midday

and by that time it was obvious that Caleb was going to need some rather more expert attention to the wound in his shoulder than could be delivered in No-Name and he decided that another trip into Rose Creek would have to be made.

Royston and Ben saddled his horse and they even offered to accompany him to Rose Creek, although it was plain that they were not too keen on the idea. Caleb gave them another five dollars with instructions that if the three decided to move on while he was away, they were, if possible, to follow and then one of them was to report back to him. They both agreed but Caleb had serious doubts as to whether or not they would follow. He felt it more likely that if the three left, Royston and Ben would also move out.

Between the three of them, Caleb's horse was coaxed and pushed across the rope bridge and Caleb rode on to Rose Creek. In No-Name wagers were being taken as to whether or not the preacher would return again or not. Royston was the one taking odds that Caleb would return and he was surprised when he had so many takers. However, if Caleb did not return then he knew that he too would have to leave pretty damned fast since he would be unable to pay his debts.

FOUR

Caleb was uncertain which was the more painful, being stabbed or having the doctor in Rose Creek attend to it. There was no doubt that the wound needed stitches but Caleb had to question where the doctor had learned the art of applying them, in fact after talking to the doctor he also began to wonder if the man was qualified in any way. His suspicions were confirmed when the sheriff told him that Doc Philips was actually the local veterinarian who, in the absence of a properly qualified doctor, also looked after the health of the human population. The sheriff also claimed that Doc Philips, the veterinarian, was far better at delivering children than his predecessor who was a proper doctor. It also transpired that the best man at pulling teeth was the local blacksmith. Caleb was quite pleased that he did not need any attention to his teeth.

Doc Philips's handiwork may not have looked too pretty but at least it served its purpose even if it did make Caleb's shoulder almost impossible to move, almost as if the arm had been stitched to his body. Luckily, the wound was in the left shoulder and for most purposes Caleb was right-handed, although he had always had a natural ability to use either hand which was why he wore two guns. As far as Caleb was concerned the fact that he would have difficulty with his left arm and shoulder presented a few problems in that he would now have to be extra careful in just how he challenged anyone.

As he left the sheriff's office after having been to see Doc Philips, he was accosted by the same two ladies who had confronted him before. The thinner of the two, the unashamed ex-slave owner, announced herself as Mrs DuPétin (pronounced Du Paytan as she took pains to point out) and that her husband had been from one of the oldest established French families in Louisiana, a fact of which she was obviously very proud. Her companion boasted the far more common name of White and could lay no claim to establishment family background.

'Reverend!' said Mrs DuPétin, plainly having to hide all her bigotry. 'The ladies of the town have had a meeting to discuss the possibility of having you perform certain...er...functions for which you appear to have the authority. I agree with everyone in that we really do need the services of a man of the church in this town and it must be said that there were a great many who were only too willing to offer you a permanent position here. However, I believe I know my fellow men...' For "men" Caleb read "blacks". 'And it is obvious to me that you are not a man who could settle in a place like Rose Creek.'

'I do believe I have already said as much,' smiled Caleb.

'Quite!' huffed Mrs DuPétin annoyed that a Negro should get the better of her in any way. 'Anyway, the point is that under my guidance it has been agreed that we are prepared to offer you a temporary appointment for three months at a guaranteed salary of three dollars a week plus a house and food...'

'Three dollars!' laughed Caleb a little unkindly, 'Ma'am, are you aware just how much I have recently earned from my shooting those four outlaws?' He paused briefly but she did not react. 'Four thousand dollars!' he continued. 'Under the circumstances I think that you must agree I certainly do not need to take up your offer.'

Mrs DuPétin simply opened her mouth speechlessly for a few moments before suddenly turning on her heels and marching off along the boardwalk as fast as she could. Mrs White on the other hand seemed full of admiration for Caleb.

'She's not going to like that, not one bit,' grinned Mrs White. 'We don't get Negroes through here all that often but when we do she always goes out of her way to make sure that they know she used to own people like them. The surprising thing is that almost always they allow her to get away with it. However, she is not the only voice on the committee and I can tell you that in the opinion of everyone else we would more than welcome your services. As she rightly pointed out, there are some things that only ordained ministers can do for us.'

'Ma'am,' beamed Caleb. 'I have no objection at all in doing whatever I can. I gather there are some weddings and christenings. The only thing I will ask is why don't those who want to get married either go to a town where there is a minister or get your mayor to perform the ceremony.'

Mrs White laughed. 'Most just can't be bothered to go and find a minister and nobody likes the idea of just letting the mayor do it, they say they don't feel married and I can understand that.'

Caleb smiled. 'Unfortunately I do have some unfinished business but I can assure you that I shall do whatever I can. If my memory is not playing tricks on me, today is Wednesday, is it not?' Mrs White nodded her head. 'I certainly hope to have my business settled in the next couple of days. In the meantime I suggest that you make the church ready for Sunday and ensure that those who require a wedding or a christening or anything else are available for Sunday afternoon.'

'I promise you a full church!' gasped Mrs White taking hold of Caleb's free hand. She suddenly looked a little nervous and glanced around to see if anyone had witnessed her indiscretion. 'Strange isn't it? Your name's Black and you are black and my name's White and I am white.' She giggled.

Caleb smiled indulgently. 'Unfortunately none of us have any control over our parents' surname or the names they sometimes choose to inflict upon us.'

Again Mrs White giggled. 'Very true, Reverend, very true. I certainly would never have chosen the name Bluebell. Yes, Bluebell White, although my maiden name was Woods which makes the name Bluebell even worse doesn't it?' Caleb assured her that Bluebell was a very nice name and she went off happily enough.

He went along to the nearest of the two saloons and ordered a Scotch whisky but was informed that Scotch was not available so he had to settle for whatever was to hand which turned out to be a very rough rye whiskey and, as was his regular habit, he casually looked about for possible outlaws. On this occasion he was disappointed in that there was nobody he could readily put a name to.

By that time it was far too late to think about returning to No-Name even if he had wanted to and at that particular moment his shoulder was still very painful and he did feel rather groggy. The owner of the saloon said that he had two rooms he sometimes rented out and that Caleb was welcome to use one for a dollar a night.

Caleb refused the services of one of the bar-girls who for once did not appear to take exception to being refused and after another rough whiskey he went round to Alma's Eatin' House and another steak, this time not quite so large. At first Alma was not so sure about serving him, fearing that he was about to shoot some more of her customers but he managed to assure her that nothing was further from his mind unless someone else chose to pick trouble with him. As it turned out he was unable to eat in peace since his presence very quickly drew a crowd of gawping youths and even some older men who wanted to see what the man who had killed four outlaws single-handedly really looked like. Caleb ate his steak and retired to bed.

Just after dawn the following morning found Caleb once again at Alma's Eatin' House for another steak. It was no use asking for anything else at Alma's no matter what time of day it was. The only concession she apparently made at breakfast was to give her customers the option of having eggs with their steak instead of vegetables. Caleb opted for a small steak and three eggs.

The inflammation in his shoulder seemed to have subsided during the night and for a time Caleb practised flexing his arm and fingers until he was reasonably satisfied that if necessary he could use his other gun.

Before he had chance to leave Rose Creek, he was suddenly accosted by a woman who told him that her father had died during the night and that it had been expected for a few days.

'It would be so nice for him if he could have a proper Christian burial,' she said. 'There was never one more regular at church when we did have a minister. Would it be asking too much for you to conduct the funeral service?'

Caleb smiled. As was normal in the hotter climates of the south and south-west, the removal and burial of a body was something which happened as quickly as possible. He gave it a little thought but reasoned that in fact he had little else to do and he agreed. The woman went off obviously delighted as she announced the news to everyone.

As things turned out it seemed that

almost the entire population of Rose Creek attended that particular funeral and Caleb felt that it certainly was not out of any regard for the deceased but out of curiosity as to how he, as a preacher and minister, would perform in their eyes. It appeared that he passed the test as everyone congratulated him. Caleb did not really mind, in fact he welcomed the odd occasion like this so that he could keep his hand in.

Even Mrs DuPétin grudgingly admitted that it was as good a service as she had ever attended but that was about as far as she was prepared to go in apologizing for her attitude in any way other than to say that she would be at church on the following Sunday.

Caleb talked with several people for a short time afterwards and it was becoming obvious that if he did not make his move very soon he would be sucked into doing a lot of things that he did not want to do at that moment. At the first real opportunity he retrieved his horse from the livery and rode out of town with some speed.

His eventual arrival back in No-Name caused a minor stir, particularly amongst those who had been foolish enough to wager that he would not come back. Royston and Ben were more than happy they had made a few dollars on the event. Caleb called Royston and Ben to what was now regarded as 'The Preacher's Room' to ask them what had been happening during his absence.

'Nothin' much,' said Royston. 'Two more rode out this mornin' an' one arrived about half an hour ago. His name's Gus Spencer, that's about all we know of him.'

'What about Porter, McCafferty and O'Rourke?'

'Still the same,' said Ben, 'they just sits an' plays cards an' share a glass of beer sometimes. They ain't said nothin' about which way they is goin' or when.'

After Royston and Ben had left, Caleb checked his Wanted posters but was unable to find anything on Gus Spencer, which did not really mean a lot. However, it was becoming increasingly plain to him that he had to do something about the three outlaws very soon. As things were they could choose to ride out at any time and he had not yet formed a plan of action. Obviously the simplest way would be to do what he had done in Rose Creek, go up to them and simply shoot them. However, his biggest fear was that if he did all the others in No-Name would try and kill him, not because they would want revenge but because they would be trying to protect themselves. He was still thinking about the problem when he went into the bar and saw the new arrival, Gus Spencer, propping up the counter.

Spencer eyed Caleb up and down coldly but Caleb detected an expert eye and was immediately on his guard as he too lounged on the counter and ordered a whiskey. The two men stood in silence for a few minutes each very conscious of the other.

'What the hell's a preacher doin' in a dung heap like this?' asked Spencer eventually. 'I hear tell you keep comin' back here which seems mighty strange to me; nobody in his right mind would want to come here twice.'

'It's full of lost souls that need saving,' grinned Caleb. 'Anyhow, I'd like to ask you the same question. Everybody else here is wanted by the law but somehow you don't look the type, in fact I'd say you looked more the type who administered the law. If you are wanted you are well off your territory, there isn't a flyer out on you as far as I know.'

'And you know about these things?' laughed Spencer.

'I've been around a long time,' said Caleb, 'long enough to recognize people for what they are more often than not. I make it my business to keep up with who is wanted by the law; I find it quite useful on occasion.'

Gus Spencer laughed and shook his head and then looked about and seemed satisfied that nobody was listening but moved closer. 'I was down in Texas a couple of months ago and I heard some tale about this preacher who supplemented his livin' by doin' a spot of bounty huntin'.' He laughed again. 'I thought it was just that at the time, a tale, but right now I'd say I've just found that preacher.'

There seemed little point in denying it and Caleb smiled and inclined his head slightly. 'And I would say I have just met up with a fellow hunter,' he said.

Spencer simply smiled and said, 'Tryin' to earn a livin' in Texas and one or two other places was becomin' almost impossible. I heard about this place from the last outlaw I met up with and it seemed a good place to earn some money.'

'What happened to the outlaw?' asked Caleb.

'I shot him,' replied Spencer in a matter-of-fact way. 'It cost me five hundred dollars but it saved a whole lot of trouble.'

Caleb laughed softly. 'Yes, I have to agree that it does make life so much easier, I tend to follow that course of action myself.'

Gus Spencer had noticed that Caleb tended to move his left arm and shoulder a little awkwardly. 'What happened?' he asked indicating the shoulder.

'It seems that someone must have thought they were in their own room and when they saw me in their bed they tried to get me out—with a knife.'

'And you convinced them otherwise?' smiled Gus.

'I never thought to ask,' grinned Caleb. 'There's two of them in a hole just up the road now. I believe their names were Sam Jones and Whispering Thomas and would have been worth about fifty dollars each so they're hardly worth worrying about.'

'Remind me to cross their names off my list,' said Spencer. 'So what do you think this place is worth?'

Caleb thought for a moment. 'Most of them are fairly small time, fifty dollars, maybe a hundred and one or two in the five hundred to one thousand range. The three big ones are Clarence Porter, Mick McCafferty and Finbar O'Rourke. I suppose those three would make up about half and along with the rest there's probably about twenty thousand dollars walking about.'

Gus Spencer inclined his head and raised

an eyebrow. 'And you were goin' to keep it all to yourself?'

Caleb smiled and nodded. 'Maybe not all of them, but those three were certainly top of my list. There's one or two who are only worth something alive and I wasn't going to bother too much about them.'

'I heard tell that there were four others in the area,' said Spencer. 'Carl Smith, Pedro Sanchez, Luke Gray an' Amos Taylor. They should fetch a thousand apiece dead or alive.'

'Not any more!' grinned Caleb. 'I'm just waiting for clearance to collect the money from them.'

'You killed 'em?' asked Spencer.

'Two days ago,' nodded Caleb.

'Hell,' grumbled Spencer, 'it's gettin harder an' harder to make a decent livin'.'

'We could clean up a nice little packet between us right here,' suggested Caleb. 'I was trying to work out how to deal with Porter, McCafferty and O'Rourke without risking getting myself killed by the others. Two of us should be able to work something out.'

Gus Spencer considered the proposal for a few moments before replying. 'I've never worked with a partner before,' he said. 'I'm a loner, always have been, even when I had me a job as a US marshal...'

'You were a marshal?' asked Caleb. He thought for a moment and then nodded. 'I suppose that makes sense. As a marshal you would not be allowed to collect any reward money and sometimes even one could be far more than your pay in a year.'

'That's what decided me,' nodded Spencer. 'I gave the job up two years ago after five years and in my first week I earned more than I did in the entire five years. Mind you, I'd had them pinpointed for more than a month. Anyhow, as I said. I'm a loner.'

'So am I,' replied Caleb. 'But look at the situation sensibly. There are at least twenty men here all with prices on their heads, as I said; there's an awful lot of money walking around out there, money that neither you nor I can collect on our own. I'm certainly not suggesting a partnership on a regular basis, just this once.'

'I'll think about it,' nodded Spencer.

'Don't take too long,' urged Caleb. 'Time isn't on our side. They could choose to move out any time.'

'Which could make things easier,' said Spencer. 'OK, I'll make a deal with you. As long as they stay in this dump and we have to take action, we share. If they move on then we're on our own.'

'Fair enough,' agreed Caleb. 'Just one thing: the two Negroes, Ben Staples and Royston Lockwood, they're working for me so don't touch them. Anyway, they are not worth a thing dead and only fifty dollars each alive.'

'I wouldn't waste my time!' grinned Spencer.

Half an hour later Caleb suddenly found himself surrounded as he leaned against the counter. He turned and saw Finbar O'Rourke on his right, Clarence Porter on his left and Mick McCafferty behind him.

'Gentlemen!' he smiled as he casually slipped his hands into the pockets of his long coat where there was a slit which enabled him to get at his guns. 'What can I do for you?'

'You can start by tellin' us just who the hell the new guy is, the one I hear is called Gus Spencer,' said Finbar O'Rourke.

'And why should I know who he is?' asked Caleb. 'I've never seen him before in my life.'

'You and him was havin' a pretty good jawin' session,' said McCafferty. 'I'm good at rememberin' faces and I've seen that face before somewhere. The only trouble is I can never remember names but I seem to remember that face and it meant trouble then and I think it does now.'

Caleb smiled and decided to play along. 'That's why I was talking to him. I too was quite convinced that I had seen him somewhere before and it seems that I was right.' He thought quickly and decided to turn Gus Spencer into an outlaw. 'His name isn't really Gus Spencer, its Gus Fogden...' Gus Fogden had been an outlaw in Texas but was now deceased, courtesy of Caleb's second gun. He only hoped that either they had never heard of Gus Fogden or at least were unaware that he was dead. 'Fogden is wanted in Texas for murder and bank robbery...'

'Yeh, that's it!' grinned McCafferty. 'Gus Fogden. Yeh, I met him once, briefly, nothin' more'n seein' him at the next table in a saloon.'

'It seems that things have got too hot for him in Texas and he's on his way further north,' added Caleb.

Clarence Porter suddenly spoke. 'Reveren', for a preacher you sure know an awful lot of folk you shouldn't oughta be knowin'.'

Caleb smiled and nodded. 'I'm not one of your regular preachers or ministers,' he said, 'I thought you might have guessed that. All most ministers want is a nice quiet life in some sleepy town where all they have to do is have matins on a Sunday morning, the occasional wedding or funeral and christening. That kind of life would bore me to tears so I try to find men and places like here. On Sunday, for those of you who are still around, I shall be holding matins in the open air outside the saloon, I do so hope you will all attend.'

The three men glanced quickly at each other and moved slightly away from the preacher. 'Er...yeh...sure,' muttered Finbar O'Rourke. 'There's just one problem, both me an' Mick are Catholics, it wouldn't be right for us to go to any other church.'

'And when was the last time any priest received confession from you?' asked Caleb. 'I would venture that it was a good many years ago.'

'When I was about thirteen,' muttered O'Rourke. 'That ain't the point though, we was still brought up Catholic and if we did meet a priest he wouldn't like it if we had to tell him that we'd been to another church.'

'I hardly think an open-air service out here would count as another church,' smiled Caleb. 'I shall expect to see you there.' He left the men and went off in search of Gus Spencer to inform him of his change in identity.

'I guess that's as good as any,' said Spencer. 'OK, I'll go along with it for now, until we've got something worked out. By the way, are you serious about the service?'

Caleb laughed. 'If for some reason I am still here on Sunday, I shall certainly go ahead with it, but I sincerely hope that by that time I shall be a considerably richer man and in any case I have promised my attendance at church in Rose Creek, that's the nearest town a little over twenty miles away. They are in the unhappy position of not having a regular minister for the moment.'

'You keep to havin' a service out here on Sunday,' said Spencer. 'It could be that we might get everyone together and maybe take them all at once.'

'Two against twenty,' mused Caleb. 'It could be interesting—stupid, but interesting. Let me assure you that those are the kind of odds I am not in favour of. I can sometimes tackle four or even five men providing there are other things in my favour. I don't know if you have noticed but I wear two guns...' He pulled aside the left side of his coat to reveal the second gun. Gus Spencer raised an eyebrow but seemed otherwise unimpressed. 'That makes three guns between us plus rifles which may not be too easy to use, especially for me. Assuming we do both of us use our rifles—mine is a ten shot—that means we have a firepower of thirty-eight bullets. The only trouble is that we can only fire a maximum of three at once, two of mine and one of yours. The outlaws on the other hand have a combined power of more than twenty shots all at once. Now, assuming that we kill or severely disable at the rate of one shot in three, that means we can dispose of eleven of them at the most before we have to reload which still leaves about another eleven men who still have a combined firepower of more than sixty shots...'

FIVE

Gus Spencer had walked away from Caleb before he had had chance to explain the pure logistics of attempting to take out more than twenty outlaws all at once. He knew the preacher was right, it would be little more than suicide to attempt such a thing and furthermore he could recognize when he was beaten intellectually.

However, the arrival of a lone rider from the direction of the rope bridge had the effect of making any plans or ideas either man may have had completely useless. The man saw Caleb and gave him a strange look and seemed to want to avoid any contact. At first Caleb did not think all that much about it and the man tied his horse to the hitching rail outside the saloon and went inside. It did not take him long to get to know O'Rourke, McCafferty and Porter...

'Are you sure?' demanded Mick McCafferty. 'I knew Carl Smith, we used to work together a couple of years ago.'

'There's no doubt about it,' said the man. 'That preacher of yours killed Carl, Pedro Sanchez, Luke Gray an' Amos Taylor almost like most men would stomp on a bug. The word is that he's a preacher right enough but that he's also a bounty hunter.'

'I should've guessed it!' snarled Mick McCafferty. 'I knew somethin' was buggin' me. All that bullshit about savin' lost souls was just talk. All he's been doin' is workin' out ways of collectin' the reward money on everybody here, especially us.'

'Then I say we just get him outside and shoot him,' said Porter.

'What about them two Negroes he has in tow?' asked O'Rourke.

'We kill them too,' said Porter, 'they sure won't be missed.'

'I hear he's pretty damned fast with his gun,' warned the man.

'He must be to take out four good gunmen,' said O'Rourke. 'We could play him along, have us a bit of fun at his expense. He don't know we know what he really is.' Just then Gus entered the room and headed for the counter. Finbar O'Rourke called him over.

'We've just had some very interestin' news about the preacher,' O'Rourke told Gus. 'It seems he ain't quite what he makes out he is.'

'He ain't a minister?' asked Gus.

101

'Oh, he seems to be that all right,' said Clarence Porter, 'but that ain't all he is. George, you tell him what happened in Rose Creek.' George was the man who had brought the news.

'He killed four men, damned good gunmen, Carl Smith, Pedro Sanchez, Luke Gray and Amos Taylor.'

'What did he want to do that for?' asked Gus pretending surprise.

'On account of he's a bounty hunter,' said George.

'Bounty hunter!' said Gus again pretending surprise. 'That sure explains why he was askin' so many damned fool questions. What do we do about him?'

'Kill him of course,' said Mick McCafferty.

Gus shrugged. 'Suits me,' he said. 'Who does it and when?'

'First one as gets the opportunity,' suggested Porter, 'I don't think it matters who the hell does it.'

'Where is he now?' asked Gus.

'Couldn't say,' said O'Rourke. 'The last we saw of him was about an hour ago. It don't matter none, all we have to do is sit here an' wait, he's sure to come in soon.'

Gus Spencer ambled up towards the rope bridge in the hope of meeting Caleb and it was Caleb who saw Gus first and it appeared to Caleb that Gus had something on his mind. He stepped from behind a rock and confronted him.

'They know who you are,' said Gus. 'A feller just rode in from Rose Creek and told 'em about you killin' them four outlaws.'

Caleb was not really surprised, he had thought that anyone coming from Rose Creek would have been sure to have heard. He remained thoughtful for a while before checking his guns and the amount of ammunition he had in his belts and eventually replying.

'I guess this means some sort of showdown,' he said. 'I suppose it had to come sometime but I would have preferred it to have been a bit later. Do me a favour since I guess they haven't worked out what you are yet, go tell Royston and Ben to be ready for trouble. I don't know if I can rely on them but apart from you, they're the best hope I've got.'

'Want me to tell 'em why?' asked Gus.

Caleb shrugged. 'They probably know already; if they don't they're sure to find out pretty damned soon.'

'And if they don't want to know?'

'Then we are on our own,' replied Caleb. 'I am assuming that you at least are on my side.'

Gus laughed. 'That all depends on what happens. If it's a case of your life or mine then I can honestly say that there's no contest.'

This time Caleb laughed. 'I suppose I can't ask fairer than that. OK, it seems I have to trust someone and it might as well be you.' He looked up at the sky and then at his pocket watch. 'It'll be dark in about an hour. I need to get to my room and get some bullets and my rifle. You just keep 'em occupied for a while.'

'And then what?' asked Gus.

'And then I don't know,' admitted

Caleb. 'The other thing I don't know is how the rest of them are going to react. It's my feeling that most of them won't want to get involved but I know that they certainly won't be on our side.'

'I'll see what I can do,' said Gus, 'but I'm not promising anythin'. As long as they think I'm one of them I'm safe.'

'Just think of all that money we stand to gain,' reminded Caleb.

'I'm thinkin' about it,' smiled Gus. 'With you out of the way it means twice as much for me.'

'Half of a lot of money is better than a bullet in the gut,' said Caleb. 'There's too many of them to tackle on your own.

'I've thought of that too,' said Gus. 'Unfortunately you're right, much as I hate to admit it. I've always been a loner and I've certainly never had to work with either a preacher or a black before.'

'And does the prospect of working with either bother you?' asked Caleb.

'It ain't never happened before so I ain't never had cause to think about it. It ain't you bein' a preacher or a black which bothers me if that's what you're thinkin'.'

'I'm not so sure about that,' said Caleb. 'Why mention it if it didn't?'

'Let's just say I could think of better partners,' said Gus. 'OK, you've made your point. I'll do what I can.'

'Don't forget to tell Royston and Ben,' reminded Caleb. 'Right now I'd better make myself scarce for a while.'

'So why should we be bothered what happens to him?' asked Royston. 'Sure, we both kinda like the guy but we're wanted too, remember.'

'There's one very good reason why you should help,' said Gus. 'I heard Clarence Porter say that they were goin' to kill you as well.'

'Why the hell should they do that!' exclaimed Ben. 'We ain't done nothin' against them.'

'That's not quite how they see it,' said Gus. 'As far as they're concerned you are in cahoots with the preacher.'

'Shit!' said Ben. 'I guess it's time we

was movin' on an' there's no time like the present.'

'I'm with you,' said Royston. 'Anyhow, why the hell should you be bothered what happens to him?'

'Let's just say that I am,' said Gus.

Royston looked hard at Gus and suddenly laughed knowingly. 'Hell, you is one too; you is a bounty hunter just like him!'

'And if you so much as say one word about it I'll make sure that my first two bullets end up in your brains although I doubt if even that would have any effect,' snarled Gus. 'And if you ride out now I'll do the same. You two are only small time, hardly worth the fifty dollars out on you. You do like Caleb says and I can guarantee that you'll be free to go.'

'If we ain't dead!' sneered Ben.

'The choice is yours,' said Gus. 'You ride out now and you will be dead.'

The two looked at each other and eventually they both shrugged. 'OK, I guess we got no choice,' said Royston. 'Just watch your back though, the both of you, 'cos if things don't go right we throw our lot in with the others.'

'I'll buy that,' agreed Gus. 'Be in the saloon in an hour and be ready.'

'Damn the man!' exclaimed Ben. 'There we was thinkin' that he had somethin' against those three like they done somethin' to his family an' all the time he was stringin' us along. I didn't think preachers an' ministers was supposed to tell lies. Hell, if you can't trust someone like that just who the hell can you trust?'

'The answer to that is simple,' laughed Gus, 'there ain't nobody in this whole damned world you can trust.'

'Yeh,' sneered Royston, 'I learned that years ago when my ma handed me over to a sheriff 'cos I stole some money from a store. She wouldn't stand for any of her family bein' dishonest even though she had sod all to be grateful to anyone for.'

'That's life!' grinned Gus. 'You just be there in an hour 'cos if you ain't I'll come lookin' for you.'

Darkness seemed to take a lot longer to

descend than it normally did and Caleb spent most of the time in his hideout above the buildings looking at his watch and glancing anxiously up at the sky. From where he was he could see everything that happened down below and he was rather surprised that activity appeared very normal.

He reasoned that he must have seen every man in No-Name by that time and he had mentally counted twenty-two different people including Royston, Ben and Gus Spencer. If his calculations were correct it meant that there were nineteen others to contend with and the possibility of one or two others he had not seen.

He lost count of the number of times he had checked his guns or his watch but eventually the light began to fade quite noticeably and suddenly darkness was all around with just a faint light on the horizon on the other side of the rope bridge. However, he did not make his move straight away, preferring to wait until it was totally dark. It seemed a long time but in reality was only about fifteen minutes.

He had seen Royston and Ben go into the saloon just before darkness fell and he had to assume that Gus Spencer had joined them afterwards; even if he had not there was nothing he could do about it. When he reached level ground, Caleb stood in a shadow and listened for a time. He saw two figures enter the building and another suddenly appeared from some bushes close by accompanied by one of the bar girls who was giggling. It appeared that she was doing a bit of private business on the side for which she would not have to account to Peg-leg. He gave them both time to disappear before making his move.

There was a rear entrance to the passage in which his room was and he had no difficulty in reaching it. A noise just inside the passage made him sink back into the shadows and only when he was satisfied that whoever it was was no longer there did he gingerly open the door.

The passageway was in total darkness and he had to feel his way to the door of his room and he had to open it quickly and step inside as the adjoining door suddenly opened and a shaft of light lit up the passage. Through a crack in the door he saw one of the girls leading a customer into a room opposite. At least that meant that one of the outlaws would be fully occupied.

He found a match in his pocket, struck it and instantly located his saddle-bags and his rifle. In the darkness he took out the three boxes of bullets he had and picked up his rifle, briefly checking that it was fully loaded and slid it into a special deep pocket he had in his coat and then slowly opened the door and eased himself into the passage.

The adjoining door had not been closed properly and through the gap Caleb could see the entire saloon. He counted ten people at the bar and five seated at tables. The five included Porter, McCafferty and O'Rourke, the other two were Royston Lockwood and Ben Staples. There was no sign of Gus Spencer.

'Damn the man!' cursed Caleb. 'Where

is he?' He waited a couple of minutes hoping that Gus would appear but he did not. He gulped slightly with apprehension and decided to go in.

Most hardly gave him a glance as he stepped into the light but Porter, McCafferty and O'Rourke sat back and leered at him but they made no attempt to go for their guns. Royston and Ben on the other hand had their hands on theirs obviously ready for action. Caleb nodded briefly at all five of them and stepped into the middle of the room, at the same time Gus Spencer appeared at the opposite door and Caleb breathed a little easier and he made his way to the counter where he ordered a whiskey, all the time expecting someone to make a move. He was more than surprised when they did not.

What did happen was Finbar O'Rourke coming across the room and standing alongside Caleb, his elbows hunched on the counter as he laughed and gazed all around the room.

'Killed any outlaws lately, Reverend?' he asked loudly. All conversation ceased and all eyes stared at the pair of them. 'Yeh,' he continued. 'I guess most of you ain't heard just what the preacher here does for a livin'.' He waited for some reaction but there was nothing more than a dumb silence. 'Our Reverend Preacher here earns most of his money killin' folk like us for money. Yes, sir, the Reverend Caleb Black is nothin' better'n a bounty hunter!'

Exactly what kind of reaction O'Rourke had been expecting was unknown, but the immediate response was an almost deafening silence followed by a certain amount of uneasy shuffling of feet.

'And what do you intend doing about it?' asked Caleb casually slipping his hands inside his coat to reach his guns.

'Hear that, folks?' called O'Rourke. 'He ain't denyin' nothin' an' all he wants to know is what are we goin' to do about it.' He sneered at Caleb. 'There ain't none of us here likes bounty hunters and I reckon the only good bounty hunter is a dead one. What am I goin' to do about it?' He stared at Caleb and slowly allowed a sneer to cross his grimy features. 'I'm goin' to kill you, that's what I aim to do about it. Any of you folk got any objections?' Again there was nothing but silence. 'There you are, Reverend, nobody raised any objection.'

'Then get on with it,' invited Caleb. 'The suspense is likely to kill me before you do.'

'I'll say this for you, Preacher Man,' continued O'Rourke. 'You've got guts, but then I guess a man needs guts to be able to stand in front of all those folk in church an' spout about lovin' thy neighbour an' all that crap. I gotta admit I'd dry up if I was put in that position.'

'You'd do fine,' said Caleb. 'Most folk think preachers talk a load of bullshit and you can certainly bullshit more than most.'

Finbar O'Rourke laughed, but he was plainly annoyed. 'I didn't think preachers was supposed to use words like bullshit,' he said. 'But then I didn't think that they was supposed to kill folk, especially for money. Just goes to show clothes don't mean a thing. There ain't no rush, we ain't goin' nowhere an' neither are you.'

'Then at least I've got time to finish my drink,' said Caleb. 'I hope you don't think I'm being unfriendly if I don't buy you and your friends one.'

'Make the most of it!' leered O'Rourke. 'I don't suppose they serve whiskey where you is goin'.'

'They certainly don't where you will end up,' smiled Caleb. He drained his glass and indicated to the Peg-leg that he needed a refill. Peg-leg hesitated until Caleb threw some money on to the counter. He picked up the glass and raised it in salute to the room in general.

Finbar O'Rourke actually seemed a little uncomfortable and certainly lost for words. He had expected a different reaction from the preacher, one which would have given him a ready excuse to kill the man—if he really did need any excuse at all. What was bothering him was uncertainty, uncertainty in that he had an idea just how good and fast the preacher was, having witnessed him in action against Whispering Thomas and at that moment he was not prepared to test himself against him. Mick McCafferty broke the heavy silence that had descended.

'Get on with it!' he barked. 'Either kill him or stand back and let someone who ain't scared do it.'

'Be my guest!' invited Caleb. 'I'm always happy to help any man on his way to the promised land.' O'Rourke and several other men moved sideways out of the possible line of fire, but this time O'Rourke turned to face up to Caleb, his hand hovering over his pistol. Caleb smiled and casually stood erect, his left hand still in the pocket of his coat from where he could reach his other gun. The flap of his coat had been pulled to one side to reveal the gun on his right hip. For a few moments both men stared at each other but Caleb was also aware of any other movements made by McCafferty or Porter.

Faced with the possibility of one of them being killed, even if the other did kill Caleb, all three slowly backed off, McCafferty and Porter moving their hands away from their guns and O'Rourke slowly relaxing, smiling thinly, and moving slowly back to rejoin his companions. As for the remainder of the outlaws in the room they apparently did not want to become involved in any way and, when Finbar O'Rourke had rejoined the other two, a semblance of normality descended. Caleb drained his glass of whiskey and ordered another and quite deliberately tempted fate by turning his back on everyone.

While this action may have appeared rather foolish, Caleb did in fact have a pretty good view of what was happening behind him through a small mirror behind the bar. Most saloons had large mirrors but not this one and that small glass over the cash drawer was the only one. It had obviously been well placed by Peg-leg to be able to see what was happening behind him whilst his back was turned.

Rather to Caleb's surprise Royston and Ben came to join him, a fact not missed by the others. Gus Spencer remained where he was at the far end of the counter although he did briefly raise his glass to Caleb in acknowledgement.

'Two beers,' instructed Caleb as Royston and Ben stood one either side of him. 'Thanks for being there,' he continued. 'I think the only reason I'm still alive is because of you.'

'We didn't do nothin',' said Ben.

'You were there, that's what counted,' assured Caleb. 'They didn't know just how you were going to act and they weren't prepared to take the chance. By the way, what would you have done?'

'Run like hell!' grinned Royston. 'I ain't never been so shit-scared in all my life. One thing's certain, you is stuck with us for the moment 'cos we just signed our death warrant in throwin' our lot in with you.'

'What about all the others?' asked Caleb.

'They sure won't raise a finger to help you or to stop anyone else from killin' you,' said Ben. 'On the other hand I don't reckon there's more'n say two or three who would be prepared to kill you, not unless you tried to kill them that is. Most is like us, petty outlaws who only stand to get a few years in jail. They probably hate your guts but they won't do nothin'. Anyhow, I reckon most of 'em is quite convinced that you're goin' to end up dead.'

'That is something which I don't intend to happen,' smiled Caleb. 'Gus Spencer is pretending he's still with them, so don't go letting on that he isn't.'

Royston glanced along the counter where Gus appeared to be in deep conversation with Peg-leg. 'I ain't so sure about him either,' he said. 'OK, so he's a bounty hunter too, but if I was you I wouldn't turn my back on him.'

'I don't intend to,' smiled Caleb.

'So what are you goin' to do now?' asked Ben. 'You can't stay here that's for sure, you're liable to get a bullet in the back any time. Us too,' He grinned and glanced behind him. 'They is tryin' to figure out just what they'll do next right now and both me an' Royston figure in those plans so where you go, Mr Preacher Caleb, we go too. You need us just as much as we need you.'

'I guess you're right,' sighed Caleb. 'It would be tempting fate too much to stay and expect nothing to happen.' He thought for a moment. 'There's a lake about a mile or so out along the southern trail. It's almost surrounded by steep cliffs with plenty of places to hole up. Get your things together and I'll meet you there. You can't miss the place even in the dark.'

'How about you?' asked Royston.

'Don't worry about me,' said Caleb. 'If I don't join you you'll know I'm dead and all you've got to do is get out of there.'

'That's for me!' said Ben. 'We could even keep on ridin','

'I can't stop you,' smiled Caleb. 'Now go get your things together while I keep them occupied here.'

'With us gone they might just try an' kill you,' Royston pointed out.

'That's a chance I'll have to take,' said Caleb, 'now get going.'

The two drank their beer and casually left the saloon and a couple of minutes later Clarence Porter also strode out fiddling with the buttons on his jeans as if going to the outside privy. Caleb was very tempted to follow but he caught the eye of Gus Spencer who indicated Caleb stay where he was as he casually strolled through the door.

'Goin' somewhere?' rasped Porter as he confronted Royston and Ben.

'Just quittin' while we can,' said Royston. Both men were aware that Porter had a gun trained on them and made no attempt to go for theirs knowing full well that they stood no chance at all.

'Too late!' grunted Porter. 'You already took sides, the wrong side. It ain't healthy to side with men like that preacher.'

'Hell, mister!' pleaded Ben. 'We ain't done nothin'. We didn't even know he was a bounty hunter until just now. That's when we decided the best thing we could do was get the hell out of it.'

'You talked to him at the bar an' he bought you both a beer,' grated Porter. 'That don't seem like the action of someone who knew nothin'.'

'That's the truth of it!' protested Royston. 'Sure, we was friendly with him, that's only natural since he's a black like us, but we sure never knew he was a bounty hunter until tonight. You won't have no trouble from us, we is ridin' out, you can see that.'

'I ain't prepared to take that chance,' snarled Porter. 'Scum like you is better off dead anyhow...'

There were two shots followed by a command for Royston and Ben to 'Get the hell out of it!' Neither man questioned the order, leapt on to their horses and left as fast as they could.

SIX

Everyone in the saloon and those still in the bunkhouses heard the shots but nobody made any attempt to investigate, all pretending that it had nothing at all to do with them. McCafferty and O'Rourke smiled but did nothing, fully expecting

Clarence Porter to walk in at any moment. Someone did walk in but it was not Clarence Porter and the only comment he made was that he had had to step over Porter's body on the way in.

O'Rourke and McCafferty almost fell over each other in their rush to get outside and it was only then that others began to show any interest as they too trooped out and stood around the body. Finbar O'Rourke knelt down and felt the artery in Porter's neck, although it was obvious from the amount of blood that he was very dead.

'Bastards!' rasped O'Rourke. 'They can run but they won't get far!' He saw Caleb and immediately his hand went to his gun but Caleb had drawn his and aimed at the kneeling man before he could even touch the handle. 'Shoot me while you can,' he sneered at Caleb. 'This is the last chance you'll get.'

Caleb backed away from the circle of outlaws knowing that the only thing he could sensibly do at that moment was leave whilst he still had the chance and at that moment it meant having to forget about recovering his saddle and saddle-bags or his horse.

At first nobody moved but suddenly, just as Caleb reached the comparative safety of complete darkness, there was a flurry of activity as guns were produced and shots began flying around. Caleb fired about three shots in response and knew that all three had either injured or killed at least one man and then he was running like a man possessed towards the trees which almost surrounded No-Name. There were several more shots in his general direction but luckily for him all were well off target and very quickly he was amongst the trees where he stopped and listened for the sound of pursuit. He could not hear any, breathed a little easier and took stock of his bearings.

Below him, Caleb could just see a few shadowy figures moving about highlighted by the dim light from the saloon and to his right he could just make out the start of the rope bridge which meant that the lake he had told Royston and Ben to meet him at was more-or-less behind him, perhaps slightly to the right. He began the slow process of climbing the steep slope and making his way to the lake.

The terrain was a lot steeper and a good deal rougher than he had imagined from the brief view he had had when hiding above the shacks earlier but eventually he did find himself standing high above the lake, having had to make one or two detours to avoid large rocks or deep ravines.

Exactly how high above the lake he was he was unable to tell; all he knew was that he was standing on the edge of a sheer drop overlooking the lake which was by then lit up by moonlight. Very slowly he edged his way to his right and round the lake hoping to find a way down.

Caleb wondered if Royston and Ben had decided to keep on riding or obeyed his instructions; if they had kept on riding he really could not have blamed them. What he was doing was certainly no problem of theirs and they did not owe him any loyalty in any way so he knew he had no right to expect anything from them. Nevertheless, he could not help but hope that they were there.

Caleb certainly did not expect them and it was obvious that they did not expect him. The first either knew about things was when Caleb found himself walking into one of them. For its part the horse responded by crushing him against the rocks and for a few minutes sportingly refused to release him. Eventually, after what seemed like an hour, Caleb was able to squeeze past the huge rump and sit down on a nearby rock and gasp for breath.

'That is you ain't it, Reveren'?' asked a familiar voice. 'It's me, Ben.'

'It nearly wasn't me,' gasped Caleb still fighting for breath. 'That damned horse tried to kill me I'm sure of that.'

'That was my horse,' said Ben rather proudly. 'She's got a will all of her own an' there ain't nobody 'ceptin me what can handle her properly an' I have enough trouble at times.'

'We wasn't sure if you were goin' to come tonight or not,' said Royston appearing as a shadow close by. 'Where's your horse?'

'Still down there,' said Caleb. 'I presume it was Gus Spencer who killed Porter?'

'We didn't rightly see who the hell it was,' said Ben. 'All we knew was that Porter was goin' to shoot us when suddenly he was the one who got shot an' somebody—we think it was Spencer—told us to get the hell out of it.'

'That was when it became obvious that my continued presence was not desirable,' said Caleb.

'What's he talkin' about?' Ben asked Royston. 'He's usin' them fancy words again.'

'I think he means he decided it was time he got the hell out of there,' replied Royston. 'Reveren', you gotta remember we ain't had no schoolin' like you so it don't do to use words we don't understand.'

'I'll remember,' said Caleb. 'I assume you are camped close by.'

'You is sittin' right in it!' laughed Ben.

'If the horse hadn't got you you'd've probably tripped over one of us.'

'It strikes me it's goin' to be a cold night,' said Royston. 'Since you ain't got no bedroll, I reckon we should light a fire.'

'And light the place up like a beacon telling everyone exactly where we are,' said Caleb. 'Don't be so stupid, I'll manage.'

'That's just like before,' said Ben. 'Three years ago he insisted on lightin' a fire and we got arrested. We managed to escape though but he still wants to light fires all over the place.'

'I like fires!' said Royston. 'The bigger the better. What I like most is seein' a whole buildin' go up. We set fire to a store in some town down south once... Wheee! did it burn but we didn't know he'd got oil an' grease stored there.'

'You set fire to it!' objected Ben. 'I never wanted nothin' to do with it, remember. All I know is we had to hightail it out of there pretty damned fast or we'd've been lynched.'

'Yeh,' laughed Royston, 'but it sure

did burn an' it sure was a pretty sight, 'specially when that dynamite blew up.'

'Take no notice of him, Reveren',' apologized Ben. 'He's just got this thing about fire.'

'I suppose we all have a thing about something,' said Caleb. 'I must confess that I am rather surprised that you are here, that you didn't just keep on riding. You had no reason not to, so why did you?'

'We thought about it,' assured Ben. 'Man, we sure did a whole lot of thinkin' all the time we was ridin'. If we hadn't found this place we would've just carried on an' not given a damn what happened to you.'

'Ben's right,' said Royston. 'We don't owe you a damned thing, in fact you've probably caused us even more trouble, O'Rourke an' McCafferty will probably come lookin' for us an' if we had one lick o' sense we'd be still ridin' like hell right now.'

'Then why aren't you?' asked Caleb.

'On account of we ain't got no sense!'

replied Ben. 'Let's just say that's what we decided to do.'

'It just seemed a good idea at the time,' said Royston. 'Thinkin' about it now it was a stupid idea, but here we is. You just tell us what to do an' we'll do our best.'

'I guess I can't ask fairer than that,' said Caleb. 'The thing is, you have the horses, you can leave whenever you like. They won't be looking for you, they think you are well away by now but they do know I don't have a horse so I am fully expecting O'Rourke and McCafferty at least to come looking for me.'

'Two of 'em shouldn't be no problem,' said Ben confidently.

'And I hope that's how it stays,' said Caleb. 'There's nothing we can do tonight so I suggest we get some sleep and see how things are in the morning.'

'We ain't much use at thinkin' no matter what time of day it is,' said Royston. 'My ma always said I hadn't got an ounce of grey matter in my head. I ain't sure what she meant by grey matter though. She used to say that about my Uncle Seth an' then she said it was brains but I saw his head split wide open by one of the white bosses an' he sure seemed to have plenty of brains then.'

'I think she meant common sense, you know, bein' able to fathom things out,' said Ben.

'Don't know about fathom things out,' said Royston. 'All I know is it does take me some time to work things out properly.'

'Exactly!' said Caleb. 'Don't let it worry you. Get some sleep and we'll talk about things in the morning.'

Finbar O'Rourke and Mick McCafferty had called a council of war in the saloon and, while almost everyone had turned up, there was obviously no appetite for a possible showdown with the preacher and nobody seemed prepared to risk their life chasing after him. The only voice which seemed to be in favour was that of Gus Spencer, or Gus Fogden as he was known.

Peg-leg had taken possession of every-thing Caleb had left behind, including his horse and already had his saddle, saddle-bags and tack on display in his store but he rarely sold such items since they were usually priced well beyond the means of the average outlaw. Actually he had deliberately priced them very high partly because of the obvious quality and partly because he had a feeling that nobody had seen the last of the strange preacher.

Gus had suggested that since Caleb was on foot, the best idea was for all of them to take to the woods in a long line and gradually flush him towards the rope bridge but even Mick McCafferty and Finbar O'Rourke were not too keen on this idea. Others were rather more practical and had decided either to leave or sit where they were, pointing out that Caleb was hardly likely to attack them since he was hopelessly outnumbered, even if he did have Lockwood and Staples to back him up.

When the meeting had come to the inevitable conclusion that nobody was prepared to do anything and that it was a case of each man for himself,

Gus announced that he was going off into the woods even if nobody else was. All thought he was mad but said that if that was what he wanted to do, it was entirely up to him.

Gus was up and on his way almost as soon as dawn broke, apart from Peg-leg he was the only person to be awake. In actual fact Gus Spencer was quite an expert tracker and very quickly picked up Caleb's trail which, to his experienced eye, was very easy to follow. Less than an hour later he was overlooking the small hollow by the lake where he could see three bodies huddled close to rock shelter and the two horses. He quietly descended, gun at the ready and stood in the middle of the hollow.

'You're all dead!' he suddenly announced. There was a flurry of activity as sleepy figures tried to find their guns.

'You were dead before you got here!' a voice boomed behind Gus. Gus simply smiled and then kicked what turned out to be a pile of brush covered in a coat.

'I should've known it wouldn't be as easy as that,' he said. 'Where were you, I never saw you?'

'I had you covered from about a hundred yards back,' said Caleb coming into the open. 'I was half expecting to have company.'

'You want to learn how to cover your tracks,' said Gus. 'I couldn't have followed a herd of cows easier.'

Caleb shrugged. 'I never was what you'd call a forest man, in fact I hate all those trees around me. So what is the feeling back there?'

'Confusion!' smiled Gus. 'That's just about the best description. McCafferty and O'Rourke are more-or-less on their own. A few will probably be movin' out but quite a few seem to think they'll still be pretty safe. There's certainly no mood to go chasin' after you that's for sure.'

'Good!' grinned Caleb. 'So have you got any ideas on what we do next? We've come this far it wouldn't seem right to simply forget it.'

'I was hopin' you had some ideas,' said Gus. He looked at Royston and Ben who were standing rather helplessly around apparently awaiting instructions. 'I don't suppose either of you have any thoughts on the matter?'

'Yeh, I have,' said Ben. 'Let's get the hell out of here.'

Caleb smiled. 'There's nothing stopping either of you, I told you that last night. There's your horses, saddle up and go.'

Royston and Ben looked at each other and shrugged. 'Where the hell would we go?' asked Royston. 'Anyhow neither of us would feel safe as long as there's still O'Rourke and McCafferty out there. They must think that it was us what killed Porter and folk like that don't forget too easily an' you must know folk always remember a black man where they can't remember a white man so it ain't so easy for folk like us to hide.'

Caleb nodded. 'I know exactly what you mean. OK, so at least we seem agreed that we have to see this thing through one way or another. How long do you think you can keep up the pretence of being Gus Fogden?'

'Until someone tells them different,' smiled Gus. What none of them knew was that at that precise moment a lone rider was heading towards No-Name who did know different.

'Well I think the best thing I can do now is to go back and take a look over the place, it might give me some ideas.'

'Go back down there!' exclaimed Ben. 'You'd be killed straightaway.'

'I meant take a look from the cover of the forest,' said Caleb. 'You two can stay here, there's not a lot either of you can do for the moment.' Royston and Ben seemed quite relieved. 'You can see if you can find something to eat. Are either of you any good at fishing?'

'I used to catch catfish when I was a kid,' said Ben.

'Then try your hand at catching whatever fish there are in the lake,' said Caleb. 'I've no idea what they are but they look big. A couple should do.'

'What about cookin' 'em?' asked Royston.

'We'll think about that when I get back,' said Caleb. 'In the meantime don't go making any fires. Do you understand?'

They grudgingly acknowledged their understanding and set to searching for some twine and a couple of stout fishing poles. The poles would present no problem and neither would the twine, hooks though were a different problem.

With Royston and Ben apparently fully occupied, Caleb and Gus made their way back to No-Name where they sat high above the buildings studying all the movements and throwing ideas about as to just how they could deal with the outlaws down there.

They must have been sitting there for at least three hours when they saw a lone rider come in from the north although neither of them gave the matter much thought other than to remark that No-Name was a whole lot busier than either of them could possibly have imagined.

Very slowly certain ideas began to

take form, chief amongst which was that if in some way they could isolate the community, somehow prevent the occupants from leaving, it would then be possible to pick off individuals at their leisure.

Whilst they were watching, they did see the now naked body of Clarence Porter being dumped into a shallow grave alongside Sam Jones and Whispering Thomas.

'We need to act pretty quick,' observed Caleb. 'Nobody will pay out if the bodies have been dug up from some grave. We need to act within the next twenty-four hours if not sooner or else Porter will be no use to either of us.'

'What we need is some dynamite,' said Gus. 'We could block off the track down the mountain and the trail just by the lake. It's very narrow there and a rockfall would mean horses couldn't get through. That would just leave the rope bridge.'

'Peg-leg seems to have most things,' said Caleb. 'You'd better see if he has some. How much money have you got?'

Gus smiled and shook his head. 'No more'n three dollars, if that.'

Caleb pulled some notes from his inside pocket and handed two five-dollar bills to Gus. 'That should buy whatever dynamite is needed,' he said. 'You can keep the change, I'll just deduct the ten dollars from your share.'

Gus laughed. 'I bet you would as well! OK, I'll see what I can do, but I don't particularly want anyone else knowin'.'

Caleb shook his head and pulled out another five dollars which he handed to Gus. 'That should keep Peg-leg's mouth shut,' he said.

Caleb had been right about one thing, the five dollars was enough to keep Peg-leg's mouth shut and yes, he did have some dynamite, pretty old stuff but still all right as far as he knew. He charged Gus five dollars for a small box containing twelve sticks.

It had been agreed that if Gus could get the dynamite he would leave it in some bushes just before the track commenced its steep, twisting descent opposite the rope bridge. Caleb saw from his lookout that Gus had apparently succeeded and, now feeling very hungry, made his way back to the lake and the hope that Royston and Ben had somehow managed to catch some fish. He was greeted by a very wet but quite happy-looking Royston.

'Two big ones!' Royston beamed as he proudly held two good sized fish, one with tail still flicking. 'All we got to do now is cook 'em.'

Caleb had to express surprise, he had not really expected anything and was quite prepared to go hungry. He looked about and eventually agreed to a fire being built under a small overhang which would dissipate the smoke. All three had said that they were not too keen on fish, but those particular ones proved very popular.

Caleb then told them of his plan to cut off No-Name and it seemed that Royston, in addition to his liking for burning things, was also something of an expert in the use of dynamite.

'Ain't nobody better!' asserted Ben. 'We

blew three safes an' hardly touched the notes inside...'

'Your posters never said nothing about robbing safes,' Caleb pointed out.

Ben laughed. 'That's only 'cos nobody don't know,' he said. 'That was before we moved up here. You gotta remember that black faces was more common down south an' to most white folk all blacks look exactly the same. Anyhow, like he says, Royston sure knows how to handle the stuff.'

'Sure do,' grinned Royston. 'I reamed it from a white man. He thought he was makin' life easier for himself by gettin' me, a black man, to blow out tree stumps for him. He collected the money an' I did all the work. He never knew just how much I reamed. You just show me what you want blastin' an' leave it to me.'

'The last time I handled explosives was in the army,' said Caleb. 'I was a lieutenant in charge of an all black unit.'

'You was a lieutenant?' said Ben. Both men seemed very impressed. 'Man, that must have been somethin' to see, a black man in an officer's uniform.'

'I wasn't the only one,' said Caleb. 'The point is that I can handle explosives if I have to but I'm not all that good.'

'Don't you worry none 'bout that, sir!' Royston gave a salute and laughed. 'Just lead us to the dynamite, show us where you want it put an' we'll see to the rest.'

'It will have to be done in the dark,' Caleb pointed out. 'And you'll have to be very quiet about it and be ready to get out of there as quickly as you can. I don't want to get this far and then have you end up blowing yourselves up or, more importantly, blowing me up.'

'Ain't no chance of that, Reveren',' assured Royston, 'but it could be that some of them down there will be suddenly sproutin' wings as they fly off to meet their Maker.'

'You just be careful,' warned Caleb. 'I don't want anyone blown up, I need bodies to claim any rewards.'

For the next few hours all three lazed about in the shade as they waited for nightfall and just before that event happened Caleb led them through the forest towards No-Name. When they arrived they circled the dimly lit buildings until they slithered down the slope to where Gus was supposed to have hidden the dynamite and, true to his word, he had. Caleb found the box and showed it to Royston who lit a match and then slowly whistled and quickly extinguished the flame.

'Man!' he gasped. 'That sure is old stuff.'

'Is it any good?' asked Caleb.

'Oh sure, it'll blow up anythin' you want blowin' up, it's just that it's old stuff an' needs handlin' with more care'n a new-born baby.'

'Can you do it?'

'Sure, I can do it,' said Royston. 'You just show me where.'

Caleb pointed almost directly above where they were at a large overhang which was at the start of the downward track. Royston looked up and studied the overhang for a few moments. Although it was dark there was sufficient moonlight to see what needed doing.

Royston tapped Ben on the shoulder and indicated that he was going to climb up and approach the overhang from the rear and whispered that he was to pass the dynamite up when he was in position. Fortunately the box also contained a coil of fuse and Royston took this with him. It seemed a very long time before a low whistle from above indicated that Royston was in position.

Three sticks of dynamite were handed up by Ben having to clamber part way up the rock face and Royston part way down. Eventually a length of fuse snaked its way down and some time later Royston appeared.

'That oughta blow that lot easy,' he said. 'There's a couple of big cracks already, it would only be a matter of time before it fell anyhow.'

'Now we place some on the rope bridge,' said Caleb. 'That's just a precaution. If somethin' goes wrong later we blow the bridge. When we are across of course.'

Royston crept towards the bridge and

examined the ropes before strapping two sticks under each of the thick main ropes, each stick being hidden by clumps of grass growing out of cracks in the rock.

'Now we go back and do the same along the trail by the lake,' said Caleb.

'I was kinda hopin' to see that lot come down,' said Royston.

'You will,' assured Caleb. 'I don't intend making a move until the morning. Too much can go wrong in the dark.'

'What do we do with what we don't use?' asked Ben.

'We have us some fun with it!' laughed Royston. 'I saw a feller blown right off his privy once. Stupid fool never told us he was in there. We was blowin' tree stumps at the time. Anyhow, he got blown right up in the air an' left his trousers behind. He warn't too bad though, just a twisted ankle an' a few bruises.'

The fixing of the dynamite to the rocks by the lake took about two hours and five more sticks which left Royston with only two to play with, for which Caleb was quite thankful.

SEVEN

Gus Spencer knew he had seen the man who had ridden in earlier at sometime in the past, but he could not remember where or when. It was also obvious that the man recognized Gus but it appeared that he too could not put a name, place or time to the face. For some time they stood at opposite ends of the counter each eyeing the other questioningly. Finally Gus simply had to find out more.

'I ain't much good at names,' said Gus, as he stood alongside the man, 'but I never forget faces. You, I've seen somewhere before, a good time ago I think, but I know I've seen you but don't ask me to say where or when.'

'Me too,' grunted the man. 'I ain't so sure that it's such a good thing to go round askin' a man who he is, 'specially in a place like this, but I gotta admit that

I'm just as curious as you. The name's Jim Cox, what's yours?'

As soon as the man said his name Gus knew that it would only be a matter of time before the man would put two and two together and arrive at the right answer. Jim Cox had been a close friend of Gus Fogden which meant that using that name would be an instant give-away. He also remembered that, as a marshal, he had been responsible for Jim Cox being sent to prison shortly after Caleb had killed Gus Fogden. Although at that time Gus had sported a full beard, Jim Cox knew his name then, which meant that using his own name now would almost certainly mean that Cox would attempt to kill him. Gus knew that in the intervening time he had altered somewhat in that he no longer had the beard but he also knew that it was simply a matter of time before his identity and his profession were remembered. He opted to say nothing for the moment in the hope that he could somehow bluff his way through.

'Jim Cox?' mused Gus. 'No, can't say

as I recognize the name, but your face is mighty familiar. Maybe you just look like someone I knew once. When a man is on the move as much as I am you see a whole lot of folk who look just like someone else. I met a woman once who was the double of my mother even as close as I am to you now.'

'Could be,' agreed Cox who, thankfully, appeared to have forgotten that he too had asked the question as to who Gus was. 'This place sure is one hell of a dump,' continued Cox. 'I know why I'm here; I'm wanted in Reno for killin' a bank clerk. Why the hell are you an' all these others here? One thing's for certain there don't appear to be a whole lot of difference between here an' the last prison I was in, both stank just the same an' the folk looked pretty much the same too.'

'Maybe that's 'cos most have been in prison at one time or another but mostly they're all here for much the same reason as you, they're all on the run from the law,' said Gus. 'Everybody here is on the run for one reason or another. It seems a good place to hole up and I don't think the law ever comes up here.'

'I've seen a couple of faces I know,' said Cox. 'Mick McCafferty for one. I'm surprised he's still alive. I did hear that he had been killed up north somewhere but if that ain't McCafferty then it's his double.'

Gus nodded and knew that he had to get out while he still could since it was only going to be a matter of time before his identity was exposed. The other alternative was to deliberately pick a quarrel with Cox and kill him. In fact that was just what he had decided to do when he was cut short as Mick McCafferty came into the room, looked at the newcomer for a second and then walked over.

'Jim Cox, ain't it?' said McCafferty as he placed himself between Gus and the newcomer. 'Last time I seen you was...let me see...' He suddenly turned to Gus. 'Yeh, that's right, you was with Gus here...'

'Gus?' queried Cox.

'Yeh, Gus Fogden, 'cept he calls himself

Gus Spencer now.'

Gus already had his gun in his hand and was ready to shoot his way out of the situation or die in the attempt but this move had been seen by another man standing nearby and before he could draw properly he felt a gun barrel dig deep into his ribs and he looked round into a leering, decayed tooth-filled mouth. There was no need for questions or answers and Gus simply shrugged, smiled and allowed his gun to drop back into its holster.

'Gus Fogden!' said Cox. 'He ain't Gus Fogden an' I oughta know; I was with Fogden for more'n three years.' A sneer crossed his face and he too drew his gun. In the meantime Gus's gun had been taken from him and held up for the others to see. 'Yeh, now I remember where I seen you before! That's where I seen your face before, you was a marshal then; it was you who had me put away. Gus Spencer...yeh...Gus Spencer, one-time marshal turned bounty hunter. Yeh, I heard you turned bounty hunter. You had a beard in them days, that's what threw me. He was the one who killed my partner at the time an' had me put inside for life, 'ceptin' I escaped.'

'Bounty hunter!' exclaimed McCafferty. 'Bloody hell, the place is crawlin' with bounty hunters!' He sneered, drew his gun and savagely prodded it into Gus's ribs. 'Now that explains a lot of things that have been happenin' round here just lately that need some answers.' He turned to the others in the saloon and called out, 'We got us another bounty hunter here, boys! What do we do with him?'

'String him up!' seemed to be the most popular suggestion.

'It ain't me who's the bounty hunter!' protested Gus in a last desperate attempt to save the situation. He pointed at Jim Cox. 'This here is really the bounty hunter...'

'No he ain't!' said one of the others. 'Me an' Jim Cox was in the same prison in Texas for two years. I can vouch for him, you don't spend two years in the same bunk room an' not know who someone is. That's Jim Cox all right.'

'I guess that settles it!' sneered McCafferty. At that point Finbar O'Rourke came into the room and immediately drew his gun and looked warily around obviously expecting trouble. 'Finbar!' laughed McCafferty. 'We got ourselves another bounty hunter. Gus Fogden here turns out to be really Gus Spencer, one-time marshal an' now a regular bounty hunter. It looks like him an' the preacher was in cahoots with each other. I thought there was somethin' wrong when he first rode in.'

Finbar O'Rourke tilted his head to one side and stared at Gus for a moment and then leered as he came forward to ram the end of his gun barrel up Gus's nose. He laughed and twisted the gun which plainly hurt which made him twist it even harder.

'I oughta ram this up your arse an' shoot!' laughed O'Rourke. 'Only trouble with that is they do tell me you don't feel a damned thing that way. I don't know how true that is an' I just might try it out on you to find out.' He eventually withdrew the gun from Gus's nose but a trickle of blood followed, some of which ran into the barrel. O'Rourke pulled on Gus's shirt and cleaned the blood off.

'I guess that explains just why he was so eager to get out there this mornin' an' go lookin' for that preacher,' said McCafferty. 'They're both in this together. He wanted to find the preacher an' plan their next move...ain't that so Mr Bounty Hunter?' He jabbed his gun into Gus's ribs again. 'What you got cooked up between the pair of you?'

'It also shows just why he was so eager to get us all to form a line an' work through the forest,' said O'Rourke. 'That way him an' his three black cronies could pick us all off.'

'Three?' queried Jim Cox.

'Yeh, three of them, four includin' Spencer or whatever he calls himself,' said McCafferty. 'The other three is blacks. The leader is a black preacher name of Caleb Black—if that's his right name—the other two are just a couple of small-time outlaws who the preacher recruited. He probably told 'em they would be confined to Hell unless they helped. Most blacks I ever met have been scared to death of religion.'

'Did you say Caleb Black?' asked Cox.

'That's what he said his name was,' confirmed McCafferty. 'The Reverend Caleb Black. I've gotta admit that he sounds like a regular minister and he wears the right clothes but that don't necessarily mean a thing; anyone can get the clothes an' a Bible but that don't make 'em regular ministers.'

Jim Cox grinned at Gus. 'Now there's another name from the past. I met the Reverend Caleb Black once, that was when he killed Gus Fogden. He tried to kill me too but I got away. Sure, he's a regular preacher right enough but he makes most of his money doin' just what Gus Spencer here does. His idea of savin' souls is to shoot 'em an' claim the reward money. Sometimes he don't kill 'em but that's usually 'cos they ain't worth nothin' dead or he's close to a sheriff. I hear he's pretty fancy with a gun too. Where is he now?'

Finbar O'Rourke nodded behind him in the direction of the forest. 'Up there somewhere. He's on foot so he ain't goin' nowhere in a hurry. Accordin' to Peg-leg it's almost impossible to even climb out an' definitely impossible to take a horse very far up there. As far as we know the other two have high-tailed it. We thought it was them who shot Clarence...'

'Clarence?' queried Cox.

'Clarence Porter,' said O'Rourke, 'He was with me an' Mick, but he got himself shot. We thought it was the two blacks but, comin' to think of it, Spencer here wasn't in the room at the time and in any case I don't think them two would have had the guts to even pull a gun on any man let alone kill him. I reckon it was Spencer who killed him.' He thrust his face close to Gus's, drew back slightly and spat. Gus closed his eyes but made no attempt to wipe the spittle away. 'It was you wasn't it?' sneered O'Rourke. Gus remained silent. 'What I want to know is just what you an' the preacher have got planned. It can't be just coincidence that two bounty hunters came here at the same time. I'll go along with any man gettin' himself lost and showin' up here, but not two bounty hunters. Anyhow, it explains just why the preacher was doin' all that comin' and goin' between here an' Rose Creek.'

'That's just what it was, coincidence, I didn't know he was here and he didn't know I was,' said Gus. 'These things happen. Anyhow, neither of us knew the other existed until we met up here.'

'These things don't just happen, not as far as I'm concerned,' sneered O'Rourke. 'Admit it, you was in this together!'

'I'd never set eyes on him until I met him here,' insisted Gus.

'Crap!' sneered McCafferty. 'You sure seemed to know all about each other pretty damned quick.'

'You just sort of get to know about these things,' said Gus.

'I reckon he's goin' to need a bit of persuadin',' grinned McCafferty. He clenched his fist and cracked his knuckles. 'I'm goin' to enjoy persuadin' him.'

'Me too!' grinned O'Rourke. 'First though I reckon we oughta let the preacher know we know who his buddy is.'

'How're you goin' to do that?' asked McCafferty.

'All we can do is march him outside an' yell out,' said O'Rourke. 'The chances are that he's probably up there somewhere lookin' down on us right now either tryin' to work out how to get his horse an' things or, more like, figurin' out just how to get at us. C'mon Mr Bounty Hunter, let's see just how good a buddy he is. If he knows you're in trouble he'll either let you rot or try an' help you. Personally I think he'll just ignore you an' let you rot.' Gus winced as his arms were twisted behind him and he was pushed outside where O'Rourke and McCafferty held one arm each. It was McCafferty who called out.

'Mr Preacher Man!' he yelled, as loud as he could. 'I reckon you can hear me. We know all about your friend Gus Spencer; we know he ain't Gus Fogden an' we know he's really a bounty hunter just like you.' He waited a few moments as if expecting some sort of response, which there was not since Caleb was at that moment eating the fish Royston and Ben had caught.

'He's goin' to die,' continued O'Rourke. 'Just like you is goin' to die. Say goodbye to your friend, Mr Preacher!' There was still no response and O'Rourke seemed rather disappointed. Gus was hustled back into the saloon where someone produced some twine and Gus's hands were pulled roughly and painfully from behind his back, his hands tied in front of him and then a rope appeared, tied to the twine around Gus's wrists and his arms were then hoisted into the air as the rope was thrown over a beam and pulled tight. Suddenly and very painfully, Gus was jerked into the air and he was forced to hang just off the floor and for a few minutes O'Rourke, McCafferty and Jim Cox walked around, each turning Gus first one way and then another. For their part almost everyone else simply stood back, some laughing at the bounty hunter's predicament and others seemingly rather bored by the whole affair. There was a couple, including the man who had confirmed Jim Cox's identity, who seemed prepared to lend their fists to what was about to happen.

During all this Peg-leg had maintained an air of complete disinterest and had ushered his girls out of the room, much to their disgust. The last thing he wanted was for anyone to know that he had sold twelve sticks of dynamite and some fuse to Gus Spencer. Whatever curiosity he had had was now pushed to the back of his mind as his own safety became paramount.

Although he was fully prepared and all his muscles were taut, the first blow delivered by Finbar O'Rourke sent a bolt of pure agony through Gus's body but there was nothing he could do to ride or ease the pain except gasp. At that point he was not prepared to give anyone the satisfaction of hearing him cry out but the second blow, this time delivered by Mick McCafferty after a couple of minutes, almost changed his mind on not crying out. The third blow delivered by Jim Cox definitely had the effect of changing his mind and this time he let out a bellowing howl of pain.

For a few minutes the blows ceased but Gus knew that it was nothing more than to allow him to recover slightly, thus making continued blows all the more painful. He had to admit that both O'Rourke and McCafferty were well versed in the art of inflicting maximum pain.

Who delivered the fourth and subsequent blows Gus had no idea. He felt blood fill his mouth and trickle down his chin and he knew that he drifted in and out of consciousness quite a few times before the blows seemed to stop altogether and he became aware of voices urging him to tell them everything he knew about Caleb and his plans. The one thing he did know at that moment was that his brain was telling them everything they wanted to know but the sounds which came from his mouth were apparently nothing but meaningless jumble.

Suddenly he felt the floor come up and hit him as the rope was released and for a few minutes he was allowed to simply lie there and he was very aware of men laughing and occasionally someone's boot would swing and sink into the softer parts of his body. After a time something cold and wet was splashed into his face and slowly but surely he started to focus on his surroundings, although at first those surroundings consisted of nothing but dirty floorboards and equally dirty boots. A large cockroach seemed to study him for some time before it apparently decided that he would make a good place to hide and burrowed under his body.

After some time one of the boots placed itself on his shoulder and roughly turned him on to his back from where he looked up into the leering face of Mick McCafferty who very slowly and quite deliberately allowed a large drop of spittle to drop on to his face. Suddenly he felt himself being hoisted into the air and when he came down again he was apparently sitting in one of the chairs with McCafferty's face close to his. He was aware of McCafferty's mouth opening and closing, but he could not hear a single word that was apparently being said, although he did not really need to hear the words to know the question being asked.

As far as he knew, Gus had said that he and Caleb had made no plans, but this reply did not seem to satisfy McCafferty whose fist suddenly slammed into his stomach again. This time he was able to fold up which in some way helped ease the pain and when he was pulled up straight he looked again into the demanding eyes of Mick McCafferty but yet again, although the lips moved, no sound came from them.

Gus supposed that he must have somehow made plain to McCafferty that he could not hear him because a jug of cold water was emptied over his head and his ears forcibly cleaned out. It made no difference as this time Finbar O'Rourke appeared to ask the same question, the lips moved but no sound came. Gus had to assume that he had replied to the question in the same manner he had before and told them that there had been no plan between him and Caleb. Again the answer did not seem to please and once again a fist slammed into his stomach.

This process was repeated several times, exactly how many Gus did not know, but at each stage the pain of the fist slamming into his stomach became less but the amount of blood flowing from his mouth became more. He passed out several times and was revived—usually by water being thrown in his face. In one final attempt to extract the information from him, Gus was again hoisted up to hang and again fists were slammed into his body but by that time there was very little sensation although he was quite certain that he had felt several ribs crack and he was also quite certain that despite his apparent numbness that he did cry out every time a fist crashed into him and he knew that his cries must have been heard by Caleb if he was anywhere nearby. Eventually oblivion came and no amount of water could bring him round.

'Is he dead?' asked Jim Cox.

Finbar O'Rourke pressed his ear close to Gus's bloodstained chest and listened, at the same time laying his hand on Gus's heart. 'I don't think so,' he replied. 'I'd say it'll be touch an' go if he survives the night though.'

'Then I say we put him out of his misery,' suggested Mick McCafferty. 'A bullet in the head should fix it.'

'It ain't like you to think about puttin' anyone out of their misery,' said O'Rourke. 'Anyhow, why waste a good bullet? A knife across the throat would be just as easy.'

'I slit a pig's throat once,' said Cox. 'It was messy, very messy, blood pumpin' everywhere. I never knew an animal the size of a pig could have so much blood. I hear that a man's got about the same amount of blood as a pig an' if that's the case then he's goin' to make one hell of a mess.'

'We don't need to do nothin',' said O'Rourke, 'we could just leave him, put him outside where the preacher can see him, maybe it'll bring him down.'

'I doubt that,' said McCafferty, 'I don't reckon even bounty hunters care a damn what happens to another bounty hunter. I know the only two others I ever knew didn't give a shit about anyone an' one killed another bounty hunter just to take a body off him which was worth no more'n fifty dollars.'

'He can still go outside,' said O'Rourke. 'The state he's in he ain't goin' nowhere an' we don't want him litterin' the floor here.'

It was finally agreed that Gus be thrown outside and left to the mercies of the cold night and possibly whatever wolves, bears or mountain lions were about.

Although not stripped of his clothes, Gus's gun, his rifle and the contents of his pockets were claimed by Finbar O'Rourke and Mick McCafferty. O'Rourke also decided that Gus's saddle and saddle-bags were better than his own and these too were commandeered.

As Gus Spencer lay in the dirt in front of the saloon, three shadowy figures passed by but did not appear to notice the body. The cold had had the effect of making Gus recover consciousness briefly and he saw the three figures but even though he felt that he had shouted out, it seemed that he was unable to attract their attention. After a few moments of trying to make his limbs and body work properly, oblivion once again took over.

'So what do we do about the preacher?' asked McCafferty. 'As long as he's out there he can pick any of us off as and when he chooses.'

'At this time of night there's sod-all we can do,' Finbar O'Rourke pointed out. 'I guess we'll just have to see what we can do in the mornin'.' He turned to the others in the room. 'How about you lot, are you with us? We're goin' out to find that damned preacher in the mornin'.'

The general consensus of opinion was that Caleb and his companions, wherever they were now, were on their own and nobody was prepared to get involved in any hunt. 'This place is gettin' too crowded!' came one observation. 'I'd feel safer locked in some jail. Most of us is for ridin' out in the mornin'. After that you can do what you like with the preacher, we just don't want anythin' to do with it.'

It appeared that of the twenty or so people in No-Name, only two, apart from Finbar O'Rourke and Mick McCafferty were prepared to stay and see an end to Caleb Black. The other two were Jim Cox and the man who had identified Cox, whose name turned out to be Sam Smith, although nobody thought that was his real name, but it never paid to enquire too closely about anyone's identity, especially an outlaw.

'That leaves just the four of us,' said McCafferty. 'I reckon we should be able to deal with him easy enough.'

'I guess it'll have to be enough,' said Jim Cox, 'but he did take out four on his own in Rose Creek, remember.'

'Then we'll just have to be extra careful,' said McCafferty. 'I'm goin' to take a looksee if Spencer is still alive; if he is he might like to talk.'

Gus Spencer did appear to be alive, but only just and he was plainly beyond being able to react or to reason. McCafferty was unable to resist kicking the almost lifeless body and he smiled with a certain amount of satisfaction as his blow brought forth quite a loud cry. He kicked again but this time there was little more than a grunt. He quickly lost interest but could not stop himself from shouting out.

'Spencer's dyin', Mr Preacher!' he called. 'What you goin' to do about it? It's just between you an' four of us now, all the others is runnin' out like the scum they are but us four will be more'n a match for you. If I was you, I'd use the time to make your peace with your Maker!'

He had no idea if Caleb had heard him or not, but it did give him a certain amount of satisfaction and helped boost his morale a little.

EIGHT

Caleb was up and about long before dawn and had still not formulated any precise ideas as to what his next move was going to be. In fact at one time he had almost reached the conclusion that the task was impossible and that the best thing he could do was to forget the whole idea. However, he had an in-built resistance to being beaten, particularly when there was so much money involved and ended up being even more determined.

Even with Gus Spencer still amongst them—or so he thought—he realized that his first idea of simply going in and forcing a shoot-out was a stupid idea as no sane man would deliberately present himself as a target and it was also a non-starter since there were just too many of them and as good as he was with a gun, he had learned from experience just when the odds might be in his favour and when they were definitely not, and this was a definitely not situation.

He struck a match and looked at his watch and calculated that there was still at least an hour to go before dawn and suddenly took it into his head to go down into No-Name and have a look about. Quite what advantage he hoped to gain by doing this was completely unknown but since he had little else to do at that moment it seemed a good idea. He thought about waking his two companions and telling them what he was doing but then decided against it and left them to sleep. He knew that they would do nothing until he returned and it was his intention to be back at dawn.

No-Name was completely silent save for some snoring coming from one of the bunkhouses nearby and Caleb had the idea of bursting in and shooting everyone inside, but there were two bunkhouses and he did not know which one O'Rourke and McCafferty were in and since they were his prime targets, he had to be quite certain and even though it was dark he reasoned that the odds were still too high should the bullets start flying about, which they inevitably would.

As he slowly made his way around the paddock, Caleb suddenly found himself tripping and falling rather noisily. He got to his knees and cursed silently as he felt around for the obstacle and drew back slightly when his hand located what was plainly a body. After listening for sounds of anyone likely to have been disturbed by the noise he made in falling and deciding that it had gone unheard, he opted to take a chance on being seen and struck a match which he quickly shook out as he recognized the bruised and battered body of Gus Spencer. Another feel of the body indicated that he was still alive.

Got to get him somewhere safe! Caleb said to himself. They must have found out about him.

The ideal thing would have been to somehow get Gus back to the lake but another feel of Gus's ribs made it quite clear that to attempt to carry him or put him across one of the horses would probably have the effect of finishing off that which the outlaws had not. He eventually decided to drag Gus across to a thick clump of bushes close to the edge of the ravine and just hope that he would be safe. He would liked to have done more for him but there was simply not the time as already there was the faint hint of dawn.

Having dragged Gus to the bushes and covered him the best he could with loose branches and leaves, Caleb decided that the time was ripe to light the fuse to the dynamite in the overhang at the start of the trail down the mountainside. If nothing else it would create a diversion and achieve the blocking off of one way down. He also toyed with the idea of blowing the rope bridge but that would also block his way out so he just settled for the overhang.

It took him quite some time to find the fuse and he had almost come to think that it had been discovered but then his hand caught it and a minute later the fuse was lit and Caleb was racing back the way he had come not caring if someone heard him or not.

He estimated that he must have covered at least half a mile before he stopped to catch his breath and as yet there had been no explosion. He had just about resigned himself to the fact that the fuse was either faulty or it had somehow gone out, when there was a sudden muffled rumble followed by the unmistakable sound of falling rock. He had heard the noise many times before and so knew exactly what it sounded like. He grinned with satisfaction and quickly made his way back to the lake.

Royston Lockwood and Ben Staples had apparently not heard the explosion and seemed completely unaware that Caleb had been anywhere and he chose not to enlighten them. They managed to rouse themselves just as dawn broke and after delousing and deticking themselves—something Caleb had done earlier—and complaining loudly about the cold, they eventually presented themselves to Caleb as being ready to do whatever he said. Caleb told them that he still had some thinking to do so Royston took himself off amongst the rocks to perform some elementary ablutions. A couple of minutes later he was racing back.

'There's a whole bunch of 'em headin' this way!' he gasped.

'How many is a whole bunch?' demanded Caleb as he grabbed hold of his rifle and started off in the direction of the trail.

'I dunno,' complained Royston as he ran to keep up with Caleb. 'I didn't stop to count, all I know is there's a bunch of 'em headed this way.'

They reached the trail and the three of them climbed a small mound, lay flat and looked down along the road from where they could now see some men on horseback slowly heading their way. They were about a hundred yards away and Caleb counted nine of them.

Caleb's first impulse was to allow the men to ride on, on the basis that it would mean nine less to deal with but as they drew closer the sight of the leading three changed his mind. To allow them to pass was going to mean watching about $5,000 being lost, the three leaders alone were worth about $3,000.

'How would you like to earn yourselves about a thousand dollars apiece?' he whispered to Royston and Ben.

'We ain't never seen that much money in our lives!' said Ben, whistling quietly.

'Well there's that much and more riding straight towards us,' said Caleb. 'All you have to do is help me kill them.'

'Man!' sighed Royston. 'We ain't never done nothin' like that before. For a minister of the church you sure are one hell of a blood-thirsty guy.' He glanced at Ben who licked his lips and nodded. 'Still, I suppose if'n it's OK for a preacher to go round shootin' folk then who the hell are we to argue? I guess the Lord must be on our side.'

'Or maybe the Devil!' muttered Ben. 'OK, we're with you...'

There was pure panic when a shower of rock suddenly rained down on the bunkhouses, more-or-less shattering the flimsy roofs and dropping down on those unlucky enough to be on the top bunks, inflicting quite a few bruises, one or two serious cuts and one broken arm. A few claimed that they had heard the explosion but to most the events had happened together and the first time they had been aware of anything was when the roofs suddenly shattered and lumps of rock descended on them.

As yet dawn still had not broken properly, there was only something of a dim glow in the hills behind them and people were racing to and fro tripping over each other, most with guns drawn and one or two even using them against imaginary targets. The horses in the paddocks charged round in sheer panic and eventually broke the flimsy fencing and raced off into the gloom. One or two of the outlaws saw this and had the presence of mind to go after the horses and in due course other outlaws joined in the hunt for them, once the initial pandemonium had subsided and everyone realized that they were not under attack.

Peg-leg stood in the middle of his empire and stared up into a large hole in the roof and swore loudly and with great passion at Caleb Black. He now deeply regretted having ever sold the dynamite to Gus Spencer but he was still not prepared to admit to anyone that he had done so. A noise in the store section of the building had him grabbing an ancient scattergun and running through. One barrel being discharged was enough to send two intruders running for their lives. It appeared that even in the midst of chaos there were one or two opportunist thiefs. Peg-leg gathered his women around him and placed himself firmly in the centre of his store determined to guard it from anyone else who dared try to steal what he considered to be his, even though most of it had been acquired by very dubious means.

As the darkness gave way to weak daylight, everyone gathered outside the damaged buildings and it was then that Finbar O'Rourke noticed that Gus Spencer was nowhere to be seen. His immediate conclusion was that Gus had recovered and somehow found some dynamite. It had also been discovered that the trail down the cliff face was now completely blocked and also that several of the boards midway along the rope bridge had been dislodged or broken and that while a man could probably get across, there was no chance of a horse being taken over.

Nine of the outlaws had made up their minds that they were leaving straightaway and it had been their intention to use the bridge and, even though it was plainly possible to repair the damage fairly easily, nobody seemed to have any interest in doing just that and the men opted for the easier way out along the trail southwards. No amount of pleading or cajoling by either Finbar O'Rourke or Mick McCafferty who were thinking purely of themselves and safety in numbers—would make them stay. In fact most of the others also said that they would be leaving as soon as possible.

'We should've made damned sure that that bastard was dead last night!' complained O'Rourke. 'Where the hell did he get dynamite from?'

'There was none in his saddle-bags,' said McCafferty. 'The only other place could've been off Peg-leg.'

'Yeh!' muttered O'Rourke. 'There's no knowin' just what he has in that store of his.' However, when they found the store owner and questioned him, he firmly denied that he had even had any dynamite. Both O'Rourke and McCafferty were far from convinced but at that moment they were face to face with Peg-leg's scattergun and took the matter no further.

The nine men who had decided to leave had by then sorted out what few belongings they had from the wreckage of the bunkhouses, saddled their horses and were mounting up. The man who appeared to have become the unofficial leader of the group advised everyone else to leave as well.

'You too,' he said to O'Rourke and McCafferty. 'Stayin' here is just plain suicide. There's a mad preacher somewhere out there an' I reckon you two are his main targets.'

'Are you scared of a preacher?' sneered McCafferty, although sensing that the man was quite right and there was little point or future in hanging about but he would not say so in front of anyone else including Finbar O'Rourke.

'I'm scared of this preacher,' nodded the man, 'an' anyone who claims he ain't is lyin' to himself. I ain't scared of facin' him but I'm shit scared when he's runnin' round like a madman somewhere out there an' causin' mayhem.'

'How'd you know it was him?' asked O'Rourke. 'We ain't seen hair nor hide of him since he took to the hills.'

'I just know,' insisted the man. 'You reckon it must've been Gus Spencer an' I admit that he seems to have disappeared, but that guy was in no state to do nothin' 'ceptin' maybe drag himself off somewhere quiet to die. No, sir, believe me, this was that damned preacher's doin', not Gus Spencer's. If I was you I'd forget your pride an' get the hell out of it while you still can.' He turned his horse and raced off with the others close behind.

They did not keep up their gallop for too long, galloping was strictly for getting out of trouble fast and no man could afford to tire his horse too quickly or unnecessarily and after a very short distance they had reduced their speed to a steady trot and felt a lot safer now that they had left No-Name.

It was questionable if any of the nine men knew what happened to them. One minute they were riding along a narrow trail feeling reasonably secure and the next minute they were falling to the ground with blood oozing from various bullet holes. Not one of them had even drawn his gun, as Caleb later discovered. In the first volley of shots the four leading riders had crashed to the ground and the rest had had to fight hard to even stay on their horses as they reared and shied. A second volley of shots sent the remainder also crashing to the ground and their horses bolted. For a few minutes there was total silence before there were three more shots as three of them tried to move. Those three shots ensured that they did not move again.

'Cover me!' ordered Caleb as he slithered down the slope. 'I'm just going to make sure they're all dead.'

'They sure should be!' declared Ben Staples. 'Man, I ain't never done nothin' like that before but I gotta admit I sure got one hell of a kick from it.'

'Me too!' grinned Royston. 'You know, I think I might even take up this bounty huntin' myself, it sure beats robbin' some out-of-the-way store or pickin' cotton for a livin'.'

'It's a damned sight harder than it looks,' said Caleb. 'You're nobody's friend and there's a whole lot of folk out there only too ready to see you dead. It's a strange thing but nevertheless very true, that most folk would rather see a bounty hunter get killed than any outlaw, no matter what the outlaw's done, and they seem to regard bounty hunting as just about the lowest way there is to earn a living.'

Royston laughed. 'That don't sound no different to the way we live now. We ain't got no friends an' there are sure a hell of a lot of folk out there only too ready to kill us, let alone ready to see us dead, so we might as well earn us a bit of decent money while we can.'

Caleb smiled and went down to the trail where he made certain that they were all dead. He did not have to shoot anyone, they had all been killed. He called up to Ben and Royston to see if they could gather up the horses and about ten minutes later they were pushing the bodies across the saddles.

'We can leave them by the lake,' said Caleb. 'They should be safe enough there and I don't think they'll be going anywhere. Now, just in case any others get the idea of leaving this way, Royston, you go and blow that rock...'

Everyone stopped what they were doing and looked towards the south. There was no mistaking it, they had all heard the shooting but nobody seemed very eager to go and investigate and they all stood and looked nervously at each other, including Finbar O'Rourke, Mick McCafferty, Jim Cox and Sam Smith.

'The preacher?' asked Sam Smith.

'That was more'n one man,' declared Finbar O'Rourke. 'Them bloody blacks must be with him.'

'Maybe it was them who got killed,' suggested Jim Cox.

'An' maybe it wasn't!' said O'Rourke. 'It was all over too quick. That was an ambush, I'm certain of that. Bloody fools, they should've stayed with us.'

'An' if we ain't careful we is likely to get ambushed as well,' said Sam Smith. 'There ain't no way down the mountainside an' right now there's no way we can get horses over that bridge. I reckon the best thing we can do is get ourselves organized an' post a couple of lookouts while the rest of us set to an' repair the bridge.'

'Good idea!' agreed O'Rourke, 'Go get everybody here.'

Actually getting everyone together proved to be a lot easier said than done but eventually and somewhat reluctantly it appeared that most were assembled and Finbar O'Rourke was just about to speak to them when there was the unmistakable sound of an explosion some distance down the trail.

'It sounds to me like they just blown the trail!' declared one man. 'Now they really do have us boxed in. We ain't got time to stand around here jawin', we've got to repair that bridge!'

'Hold on!' commanded O'Rourke. 'We've got to get ourselves organized an' we have to post some lookouts. I want three volunteers!'

'You, McCafferty an' Sam Smith!' jeered another man. 'Come on!' he urged the others. 'We got us a bridge to mend an' get across.' Everyone seemed in total agreement and O'Rourke, McCafferty, Smith and Cox were forced to stand by and watch as all the others seemed to get in each other's way. Eventually Finbar O'Rourke shrugged his shoulders and told his companions to go and take up positions where they could watch for possible intruders.

From his vantage point overlooking the lake, Caleb surveyed the blocked trail with a feeling of great satisfaction. The explosives had apparently been well placed and a very large section of rock had slipped down and now completely blocked the narrow pass. Now there was only one way around the blockage and that involved a swim in the lake which, at that point, meant going down a steep and very rough slope of about twenty feet and ending up in water of at least that depth again. It certainly was not completely impassable but in his experience most outlaws and even law-abiding citizens out West could not swim. In any case he did not really expect anyone to attempt this way out, the blocking of the trail was just a precaution.

The bodies of the nine outlaws had been laid out under an overhang of rock and their horses tethered nearby and with so many out of the way, Caleb began to feel rather more adventurous although he was still not prepared to simply ride in and force a gunfight with outlaws of largely unknown abilities in the use of guns. He felt that rather like cornered rats, such men were probably at their most dangerous in such situations.

'What next?' asked Royston. 'We gotta act soon 'cos they is probably even now gettin' their horses across that bridge.'

'Just what I was thinking,' agreed Caleb. 'Maybe I should've blown the bridge as well.'

'What you mean?' demanded Ben. 'As

well as what?' Caleb smiled and told them what he had done earlier at which both complained loudly that they should have been there.

'Man!' sighed Royston shaking his head rather sadly. 'I thought you was a man of learnin', you know, a man who knew what he was about on account of he had some proper schoolin'. What you wanna leave the bridge for, they'll all be gone when we get there?' Caleb had to admit that he had probably been wrong and his only defence was that he had been thinking about how they would be able to get out of there. Royston laughed. 'I would've thought that wouldn't've mattered. If they was all dead we could've worked out some way to get out.'

'Well let's get going,' said Caleb, 'I see you both managed to get better guns; I hope you can use them as well as you did your old ones.'

'Don't you worry none about us,' declared Ben. 'We can handle ourselves; you just tell us what you want us to do an' we'll do it.'

'That all depends on what we find down there,' said Caleb.

What they did find as they looked down from the safety of the trees were men running to and fro with timbers and ropes apparently repairing the bridge. A sudden movement a few feet below them revealed a figure crouched apparently on guard. Caleb, who had seen the man, nudged his companions and pointed and then raised a finger to his lips to indicate silence. He scanned the bushes and located two more figures.

'Have you ever slit a man's throat?' Caleb whispered. They both shook their heads. 'Well now's the time to learn,' Caleb continued. Both men looked rather nervously at each other for a moment and eventually nodded their agreement and took out hunting knives which they always carried and tested the sharpness of the blades on pieces of grass.

'How about you?' asked Ben.

Caleb smiled and shook his head. 'It's the first time for me too!' he said. 'Royston, you take the one just below us. You should be able to get round the back of him easy enough if you go that way...' He indicated to his right. 'Ben, you take the one over there, you should be able to get behind him too. I shall take that one over by that thorn tree. I shall need some time but don't let that stop you. When you've done it just stay where you are until I call you or until something happens.'

'An' dependin' on what happens means we either get the hell out of it or start shootin',' said Ben.

'Something like that!' grinned Caleb. 'Now, just give me a couple of minutes before you move.' He disappeared down a very narrow but quite deep gully which seemed to lead down to where the third man was but suddenly found himself almost at the back of a fourth figure, although he was not one Caleb immediately recognized, certainly not Finbar O'Rourke or Mick McCafferty. The man obviously either heard or sensed that someone was behind him and he turned and fired in the same instant. Fortunately for Caleb he had ducked behind an old tree stump and the shot simply smashed into the stump.

There was no time for thinking and Caleb reacted purely by instinct and his single shot brought a deep red mark to the man's forehead from which only a thin trickle of blood managed to ooze. Although staring straight ahead the man plainly had no further interest in his surroundings. Caleb moved forward and touched the body which slumped to one side, having been supported by a rock.

The effect on the other three lookouts was instant as each suddenly took to their feet and were running down the rough slope towards the buildings. It had also been as much of a surprise to Royston and Ben and they were slow to react, although Ben did claim that he had managed to hit one of them.

Everyone down below heard the shots and for a few moments all work on the bridge—which was almost finished —stopped and guns were drawn and defensive positions taken up. When Finbar O'Rourke, Mick McCafferty and Jim Cox were questioned, they were all forced to admit that they had seen nothing and that they had only been interested in getting away.

It was agreed that six men should take up positions to repel any attack whilst the others, four in all, should continue with the repair.

High above, Caleb noted what was going on and began to make plans accordingly.

NINE

Caleb rejoined Royston and Ben, both of whom seemed quite disappointed at not being able to carry out their allotted task, and Caleb was forced to remark that it was strange how they had suddenly been converted from men who had not wanted to be involved in killing in any way to seemingly bloodthirsty hunters.

'I think it is more than possible that the prospect of a thousand dollars has something to do with it,' suggested Caleb. 'You both said you had never seen so much money in your lives.'

'I'd say it has one hell of a lot to do with it,' agreed Royston. 'When we was on the run from the law ourselves the idea never really crossed our minds. Things like that don't come into it when your own neck is on the line.'

'So what changed your minds?' asked Caleb.

'We decided that it paid better, just like you found it paid better'n just bein' a minister,' grinned Ben. 'OK, so what do we do now? It looks like the bridge got busted an' they're repairin' it. There's still at least ten of 'em down there, we just took out nine so one more shouldn't be no problem.'

'That was completely different,' said Caleb. 'Ambushing nine men is one thing but they know we're here now and they're ready for us, so it won't be easy. We can't shoot them from up here, they're well out of range of handguns and it's a question if even a good rifle would have much effect.

No, we have to get closer, even amongst them. It looks like they've almost mended the bridge and once they get across we can safely say we've lost them. I know this sounds crazy, but what we have to do is blow that bridge again. I don't know if they've found the dynamite we strapped to it, we just have to hope they haven't, but I don't think they have. One of us has to get in there and light those fuses.'

'You is damned right about it bein' crazy!' laughed Ben. 'OK, so we bring the bridge down again, how the hell do we get out?'

'With difficulty!' smiled Caleb. 'But like you said before, if they're all dead we have time to figure that out but first we have to deal with them and then we think about just how we're going to get out, remembering that if we do succeed in taking them all out we are going to have about twenty bodies to get out as well. We still have to bring the bridge down and the only way to do that is to create a diversion so that one of us can get to it and light those fuses.'

Royston grinned and pulled two sticks of dynamite from inside his shirt and held them for Caleb to see.

'These two in the right place should give 'em somethin' to think about,' he suggested. 'Maybe, if I could get close enough, I could throw one on to the bridge, that way we don't have to get too close.'

Caleb smiled but shook his head. 'The idea is sound but the trouble is I don't think it will work. The chances are that if you throw it it is likely to miss the bridge completely or it will just roll between the slats and fall into the ravine that way. No, we have to light the fuses on the dynamite already there somehow.'

'Well we'd better do somethin' pretty damned quick,' said Ben. 'It looks like they've finished. Look, a couple of 'em are already takin' their horses to it.' Ben was quite right, in fact four or five were in the process of leading their horses out towards the bridge.

'OK!' said Caleb. 'Royston, you make your way round that way...' He indicated his left. 'Throw the first one into what's left of the store and then try to throw the second as close to the bridge as possible. That ought to make them back off for a while, at least long enough for either me or Ben to get to the bridge where one of us can hold them off as best we can while the other lights the fuses.'

'Sounds fine to me!' agreed Royston. 'It's just a pity we don't have more, I could really make 'em panic.'

'The idea is to make the horses panic,' said Caleb. 'That'll be enough to keep them occupied for a while.'

'Then what are we waitin' for?' grinned Royston. 'See you at the bridge!'

Royston disappeared amongst the trees and Caleb and Ben made their way round in almost a semi circle towards the bridge. It took them about five minutes to get into position amongst a thick clump of bushes no more than twenty yards from the bridge but there had been no sound from Royston and they were both beginning to think that perhaps he had not made it when suddenly there was a deafening explosion and pieces of shattered timber flew into the air closely followed by loud screams from the women.

For a brief instant everyone stood still but once the initial shock had passed and even before loose timbers had stopped falling, three men were forcing frightened horses on to the bridge. Caleb cautioned Ben not to make a move which was perhaps as well since the other stick of dynamite exploded close to the bridge. The explosion seemed to badly injure at least one horse and one outlaw but the three horses and men already on the bridge somehow stayed on despite the bucking and stamping of terrified animals. Those who had been closest to the bridge who had not been injured were dragged away by their horses. Caleb touched Ben and they broke cover, although nobody seemed to notice them in the general pandemonium.

Caleb indicated that Ben should light the fuses while he crouched behind an injured horse and began shooting at anyone within range and sight. As far as he knew he injured at least two and possibly killed one, but he could not be certain.

Ben flattened himself on the ground and fumbled under the ropes of the bridge and found one of the sticks of dynamite which he lit and he then scrambled to the other rope but a sudden hail of bullets raising the dust all round him forced him back to Caleb. Caleb had seen the man responsible for shooting at Ben and had easily identified him as Finbar O'Rourke, and he had managed to force him back by emptying both his Colts in his direction but he knew he had not hit him. Ben indicated that he had lit one fuse and that they had better get out of the way quickly. Caleb nodded and both suddenly made a dash from behind the injured horse, across the twenty or so yards to the bushes and then into a narrow gully where they waited, heads and ears covered.

The explosion, when it came, seemed a very weak affair but when Caleb raised his head he was quite satisfied with the result. He had just been in time to witness the three horses and outlaws who had been on the bridge disappearing into the depths of the ravine. Those were three bodies he would have to find later. The explosion had ripped out one of the moorings of the bridge and it was now held at the far side only and by one anchor point on their side, leaving it swaying drunkenly with most of the slats having also disappeared into the ravine, but at least it was possible to repair it.

Quite suddenly a heavy silence descended, a silence broken only by the occasional frightened neigh of a horse. Apart from a few horses, nothing moved and Caleb was able to take some stock of the carnage. According to his calculations three men had perished in the ravine, one he had shot earlier and there were now three more bodies lying fairly close by, that made seven. There were at least another two, possibly three or four, he just did not know and at that moment he did not think it wise to venture from cover to find out.

A lone figure suddenly staggered from the wreckage that had been the saloon clutching a scattergun in one hand and a pistol in the other. For a couple of minutes he swayed unsteadily and looked about as if challenging anyone to show themselves. Peg-leg slowly hobbled towards the bridge where, for a few moments he swayed unsteadily on the edge of the ravine before he started calling.

'Where the hell are you? Come on out you damned preacher, I know you're there somewhere. Come on out and face me like a man. You've just destroyed years of hard work. Damn you, Caleb Black! Damn you, damn you!'

Actually Caleb felt quite sorry for the man and his women who had now also emerged from the rubble, their dresses tattered and torn and stained with blood, but they did not appear to be too badly injured. Another figure appeared behind what had been the saloon and was plainly Royston Lockwood but hardly had he shown himself when he was sent crashing to the ground by a single shot. Peg-leg immediately swung round and discharged both barrels of his scattergun in the general direction of the shot, but to no avail. Caleb too looked in that direction and was in time to see two figures running into the forest. He waited another five minutes, during which time there were no movements other than Peg-leg staggering drunkenly and it was then that Caleb realized that part of his wooden leg was missing. Eventually Caleb nodded to Ben and they slowly ventured out into the open.

'Bastard!' snarled Peg-leg when he saw them and raised the scatter-gun.

'You haven't reloaded,' Caleb pointed out as he too raised his rifle. There was a click as Peg-leg squeezed one of the triggers and nothing happened. 'Told you so,' said Caleb. 'Now don't be stupid, I have no argument with you, I don't want you.'

'For a man who don't have no argument you sure have one hell of a strange way of showin' it,' hissed Peg-leg as he lowered the gun. 'OK, I know when I'm beaten, but you still ain't caught the main two you was after. That was O'Rourke an' McCafferty high-tailin' it into the forest.'

'I thought it might be,' sighed Caleb. He

turned to Ben. 'You'd better go and take a look at Royston.' Ben needed no second bidding and raced off to find his friend. 'I had hoped they would be dead,' he said to Peg-leg, 'it would have made life so much easier, but life is rarely that easy.'

Ben came back looking reasonably happy and announced that Royston would be suffering with a headache for a few days and that he had only suffered a grazed scalp and that it would have to be a pretty hard bullet to penetrate such a thick skull anyhow. Royston proved that he was still alive by standing up and rubbing his head.

For a few moments it looked as if Peg-leg had changed his mind and was going to force a showdown and it took his women to surround him and take his guns away and lead him to the one shack that still had four walls standing where they set about tending his wounds. Caleb took the opportunity to look at the bodies and make a note of who everyone was as best he could and to put a value on each one. After ten minutes he decided that Peg-leg had been right and that it was Finbar O'Rourke and Mick McCafferty who were out in the forest somewhere. Who the three were who had perished in the ravine he was not sure, the only thing he knew for certain that none of them was either O'Rourke or McCafferty. The carnage had been almost complete in that all except two outlaws were dead and accounted for: nine who were up at the lake, Clarence Porter who had been killed earlier and was at that moment buried close by, one he had killed just before they had attacked, three now at the bottom of the ravine and a total of five now lying close by—plus of course Finbar O'Rourke and Mick McCafferty who had unfortunately managed to escape. Jim Cox was one of the bodies lying nearby and together with the other four, Caleb added another three thousand to his grand total. However, he still needed O'Rourke and McCafferty to make it a very profitable exercise.

He suddenly remembered Gus Spencer and ran to the clump of bushes where he had left him and, somewhat to his relief, he discovered that Gus was still alive although unconscious but with a left leg which looked decidedly unhealthy and was at that moment crawling with maggots. He called one of the women and ordered her to clean up the leg. Gus was dragged to the shack and Caleb called Ben and Royston and told them to gather all the bodies together, including those from the lake and Clarence Porter from his grave. They did not seem too willing to dig up a grave fearing the wrath of evil spirits, something they still believed in even after years away from the influence of black superstition.

It was their considered opinion that Caleb was completely mad to want to go after the other two outlaws and announced that they had no intention of going with him since, as far as they were concerned, they had had more than enough excitement for one day.

Caleb had seen Finbar O'Rourke and Mick McCafferty take to the forest and, although he was not too fond of such places, always having the feeling that the trees were about to fall down on him at any moment and a very definite fear of meeting large bears, he felt that he did have a certain advantage over the two outlaws in that he had also been forced to spend some time in the forest and thought that he knew the area pretty well.

Caleb soon found that even his untrained eye could follow the progress of the fleeing pair quite easily. A trail of broken branches, trodden down grasses and quite a few footprints in the boggy ground guided him unerringly and they appeared to be running into what he knew was a high, almost sheer wall of rock. He decided to slow down and proceed with more caution since it was highly likely that he would come across them quite suddenly.

The trail suddenly ceased at the wall of rock and whereas a trained eye would probably have been able to simply examine the smooth rocks he was now faced with and know which way the outlaws had gone, to him one rock and all its scratches and markings looked exactly the same as the next.

It would have been much easier had Caleb been prepared to venture from the comparative safety of the trees and examine the rocks in greater detail but that meant exposing himself in full view and presenting a very easy target to even the poorest of marksmen. He sat on a fallen tree and studied the rocks for quite some time and each time he looked at a particular rock he imagined that he could see clear signs of someone having clambered across the smooth surface, but when he looked at that same rock again a few minutes later he was equally convinced that the signs indicated the opposite direction. Yet again he could not be certain that there were any signs at all. Eventually he sighed with disgust and vowed that he must learn the art of tracking someone properly. He had often marvelled at the abilities of others in this field and he had met one or two whom, he had been convinced, could even follow a fish through water.

For a time he sat and listened. He had always prided himself on being able to hear the slightest sound from quite some distance but now he found that either his ears were playing tricks on him or he was beginning to imagine sounds. The sudden flight of a bird close by had him leaping to his feet and aiming his rifle but he was saved from giving away his position by the realization that it had been nothing more than a bird. He settled down again to listen and think.

The stark fact was that he was faced with two choices; he could go either left or right. Going up had crossed his mind briefly but a closer look at the rock face convinced him that no normal person would be able to climb it and certainly not him. He was about to move when he suddenly realized that in his haste he had forgotten to reload his two Colts and he spent a couple of minutes correcting that oversight.

Since it did not really seem to matter which way he went, he decided to head to his right which was slightly uphill, although he took care to keep to the cover of the trees wherever possible which, the further he went, proved more and more difficult. After about ten minutes he found himself facing a large, smooth, expanse of rock about fifty yards across. He did investigate a little further down but discovered that it ended in a sheer drop of at least 200 feet. It was here that he once again saw firm evidence that someone had passed that way quite recently in the form of two different footprints in a piece of boggy ground and some crushed grass. He sank back into the cover of the trees once again and studied the situation.

The far side of the flat rock seemed to be littered with ideal places for anyone to hide and to ambush him and he wondered if he had been seen or not, although he had tried to keep to cover as much as possible. He spent another fifteen minutes simply sitting, looking and listening. Suddenly he knew that his patience had paid off.

The figure of Finbar O'Rourke suddenly appeared at the far edge of the rock about fifty yards away from where Caleb now was and so way beyond the range of his Colts and even though within range of his rifle, any shot would have to be extremely accurate—probably too accurate for him at that range—or remarkably lucky.

O'Rourke knelt down and scooped up some water from one of the many small streams of water running down the smooth rock and appeared to be looking about, although it was obvious that he was unaware of Caleb on the other side. There was no sign of Mick McCafferty, something which Caleb found rather puzzling, but he had to assume that both men were still together. After about five minutes O'Rourke made his way back into the jumble of large fallen rocks and bushes but, try as best he might, Caleb was unable to keep track of him. However, he felt that apart from waiting until it was dark, that moment was probably the best opportunity he would have to cross.

A few seconds later Caleb was running as fast as he could across the smooth surface, slipping once but regaining his feet very quickly and he reached the far side without incident, where he sank breathlessly behind a large rock to wait and listen. How long he waited he did not count, but it seemed rather a long time.

Eventually he stood up and peered around the rock, first to his left and then to his right, all the time listening for sounds of men moving. The only sounds came from the steady streams of water or from birds and insects and even he, as inexperienced as he was in such things, was learning what was a natural sound and what was not. He slowly moved out, rifle at the ready, and cautiously made his way between rocks and bushes in the direction Finbar O'Rourke had taken.

The stretch of rock and scree he was now crossing was, in fact, quite narrow and appeared to be the result of some ancient rock fall and he was suddenly faced with an almost identical situation as before. Another large, smooth expanse of rock, again about fifty yards wide, faced him, although this time there was more water flowing down it in fact a good stretch of the central part of the rock was taken up by what appeared to be a fast flowing river, although plainly very shallow. The one main difference between this section of smooth rock and the one behind him was that there were several bushes clinging precariously to cracks in the rock, but at least they provided some form of cover. Where O'Rourke had crossed was impossible to tell since any wet footprints had been very quickly dried by the heat of the sun which was by this time quite high in the sky. Once again the rock ended in a sheer drop.

This time the far side was a cliff face about a hundred feet high which seemed to be a semi-circle ending at the rough section where he now was. A waterfall cascaded down on to the flat rock drowning out any sounds he might hear so his next move depended very much on sight and pure guesswork. However, one thing he did not have to guess at was exactly where Finbar O'Rourke and Mick McCafferty were.

On the far side, overlooking the flat rock, there was what appeared to be a cave and suddenly two figures moved in the entrance and there was no mistaking just who they were. The figures stood and looked for a few minutes but did not give the impression that they knew the preacher was there and eventually they disappeared back into the cave. Caleb moved instantly.

The first of the bushes was only about ten yards away and he made its protection quite easily. The next was at the edge of the water and that too was easily reached. It appeared to be the next bush which would prove the most difficult, standing as it was in the middle of the river.

He ran towards the bush and had almost reached it when he suddenly found himself sliding on the wet, slimy surface of the rock and could not prevent himself from falling. The force of the rushing water and the slippery surface made him slither downwards and he was heading quickly towards the end of the rock. His one chance to stop himself appeared to be a small bush, again almost in the middle of the water and in desperation he grabbed at it and, miraculously and much to his relief, the bush was well anchored and took his weight. He looked downwards and grinned as he realized he had been a matter of a few feet away from disappearing over the edge. Somehow, in all this, he had managed to hold on to his rifle.

Very slowly, not daring to put too much pressure on the stem of the bush, he managed to find a foothold and ease himself upwards and eventually, after what seemed like hours, he was able to sit up with his legs either side of the bush. He looked across at the cave but it appeared that his ungainly descent had gone unnoticed and he prepared to make the final crossing to the drier part of the rock.

That appeared easier said than accomplished since he still had about ten yards to go with no obvious footholds or bushes to help him and this time one slip would almost certainly mean him going over the edge and certain death. He gulped and stood up a little unsteadily and slowly and agonizingly made his way across. That ten yards was the longest ten yards Caleb had ever undertaken.

Eventually he was on dry rock but feeling decidedly groggy and was forced to sit down under the cover of a large rock and rub some feeling back into his very wobbly legs. He was actually very surprised that his very ungainly crossing had apparently gone unnoticed. Although at the time his one concern had been avoiding killing himself, he would not have been surprised to have seen either or both outlaws standing waiting for him or even helping him on his way.

TEN

In actual fact Caleb was a little too complacent. Although he had not actually been seen, his descent and eventual dash to safety had been heard by Finbar O'Rourke although, fortunately for Caleb, immediate sight of what had happened had been obstructed by several large rocks and at that moment the two outlaws were on their way down to investigate.

It seemed to be pure chance which made the two reach the edge of the large flat rock a few yards below where Caleb was recovering. They could quite easily have chosen a route which would have come out almost on top of Caleb and he would have stood little chance of protecting himself. As it was, he heard rather than saw the two men and managed to draw himself into the cover of a bush before they appeared.

Even before he had seen them, his rifle was at the ready and as soon as he saw them he made a snap decision. His rifle was at his shoulder and automatically he fired bringing down Mick McCafferty, who was the nearest. However, Finbar O'Rourke reacted very quickly and before Caleb could shoot again he was diving for the cover of a nearby rock and then returning fire.

Caleb was satisfied that McCafferty was dead, he had never yet missed a target from the twenty feet or so he had been from him. He could see a thin trickle of blood oozing from a hole in McCafferty's tight temple and called out to Finbar O'Rourke.

'There's just you and me now, in a short

while there's just going to be me.'

'How the hell did you find us so quick?' demanded O'Rourke. 'I checked back not so long ago and there was no sign of you then.'

'I know, I saw you,' laughed Caleb. 'It seems to me that your woodsmanship is worse than mine and that's got to be pretty bad. Your trail was easy to follow.'

'I'll say this for you, Mr Preacher Man,' called O'Rourke, 'you sure are persistent. If anyone had laid odds that you could have done half of what you have I wouldn't have taken them. Did you kill all those who left early this mornin'?'

'Sure did!' laughed Caleb. 'All the others are dead now as well, all except one and I intend to correct that little oversight very soon now.'

'Not if I have anythin' to do with it,' replied O'Rourke. 'You could never've done it on your own though, you had those other two blacks an' Gus Spencer helpin' you.'

'Gus Spencer had nothing to do with it,' said Caleb. 'I managed to hide him before

I blew that rock. He's still alive, at least he was when I came after you, but he looks to be in a bad way and it might be touch and go if he does survive.'

'I hope the bastard dies!' snarled O'Rourke. 'I should've finished him off last night. So what do we do now, Mr Preacher?'

'It would appear that we do have something of a stand-off,' agreed Caleb. 'The fact is that I intend to kill you; I have never found it worthwhile to attempt to take in prisoners alive. Obviously it is your intention to kill me too, so either way one of us is going to end up dead, so I suggest that we settle it once and for all.' All the time he had been talking, Caleb had been very slowly edging himself around the rock he was now behind and since he was doing so, he guessed that O'Rourke was probably doing the same and a very slight change of direction of his voice confirmed this.

'Stand an' face each other you mean?' called O'Rourke. He laughed derisively. 'The one thing I've learned in life is never face a man in a draw. I may be faster than you and you may be faster than me and that's a risk I'm not prepared to take. This may take a long time but I intend to stay alive and kill you.'

'If that's the way you want it, that's fine by me,' replied Caleb. He had not been too sure about facing O'Rourke anyway, since he had never considered himself particularly fast on the draw. His main attribute was in being able to use either hand and making people think that they had the drop on him when he used his right hand. He would casually reach beneath his coat and use the gun on his left thigh. On this occasion he did not think such a strategy would work. He looked upwards...

Both men lapsed into complete silence as each attempted to get the better of the other. Finbar O'Rourke had apparently made better progress than Caleb and he flattened himself against the rock quite certain that Caleb was on the other side. As he eased himself round he suddenly felt the barrel of Caleb's Colt jab into the top of his head. The last words Finbar O'Rourke ever heard were 'Goodbye Mr O'Rourke!'

Caleb had never actually shot a man from above before and certainly not from such close quarters. The shot seemed to make O'Rourke's skull shatter rather like smashing a water melon and even his hardened stomach revolted a little. He clambered down from the rock and looked about for some easy way of dragging the bodies across the flat rock and the fast running water without risking losing both them and himself over the edge. He eventually found a point which was not so slippery and far enough away from the edge and dragged the bodies, one at a time, across, where he decided to leave them and return to No-Name for a horse on which to transport them the remainder of the way.

Finding his way back was easy enough but by that time it was close to nightfall so he had to abandon any idea of returning that day. In the meantime Royston and

Ben had completed the task of collecting all the bodies although they had not removed Clarence Porter from his grave and Caleb was forced to do that unsavoury task. When he had, he told them to find a shirt and jeans to put on the dead man.

Caleb's next task was to recover his saddle and saddlebags and find his horse, although there were plenty of other horses to choose from, it was just that he was used to his own animal.

The three of them surveyed the bridge and discussed ways of repairing it but they eventually decided that it would take too long and that the easiest way would be to clear a way through to the trail down the mountain. Royston and Ben wanted to leave this job until the morning but Caleb insisted that they tackle it straightaway. In the event it needed a couple of hours the following day, a job he left to Royston and Ben while he returned to collect the bodies of the two outlaws.

The journey down the mountain trail was rather hair-raising, at least to Caleb,

Royston and Ben. The horses, as horses always seem to be, were oblivious to the dangers and hardly put a foot wrong. The trail was very narrow with a drop of more than 500 feet in parts and they had ten horses in tow, all except one carrying two bodies. Gus Spencer had been put on to one horse, supported as best he could be and they knew it would be more a matter of luck than judgement if Gus ever made it to Rose Creek alive. If he did, Caleb hoped for Gus's sake that the veterinarian, Doc Philips, would be able to do something for him. More than once Caleb thought that they were going to lose one or more of the horses, as well as himself, but eventually after a very slow and dangerous descent, they reached flat ground.

Much to Royston and Ben's dismay, when they did reach level ground, Caleb insisted on following the course of the river looking for the three men who had fallen off the bridge. That particular task took most of the day but they found two of the bodies quite easily, washed up against rocks. The third they eventually discovered

220

in the branches of a tree almost directly below the rope bridge swinging high above them. It took almost an hour to get him down at which point Caleb suggested that they make camp for the night.

They had left Peg-leg and his women to make their own arrangements, although by that time Peg-leg was talking about rebuilding his saloon-cum-store and repairing the rope bridge. The only comment Peg-leg had made when they had left was that one day he intended getting even with Caleb.

Caleb had not seen anyone on their way to Rose Creek, but shortly before they even saw the town, it appeared that several of the residents had somehow heard about this strange caravan and had ridden out to meet it. There were about twenty of them in all and although there were a couple of curious questions, most seemed content to simply ride alongside and escort them into Rose Creek. The one comment that everyone made was about the vast number of flies which accompanied the bodies.

Caleb was not surprised at all. Even in the most remote parts of the desert, it seemed that flies were suddenly brought to life by the smell of blood. Royston and Ben had attempted to waft the flies away in the early stages but they had had to concede that it was a pointless exercise, even in the case of Gus Spencer.

As they came closer to Rose Creek so other curious citizens joined them along with yapping dogs, some of which seemed quite excited by the smell which came with the line of horses. There was even a solitary pig which seemed to think of itself more as a dog than a pig. The reception committee in Rose Creek was even larger and included the town mayor, the sheriff, Mrs Bluebell White and, of course, Mrs DuPétin. Of all of them, the sheriff appeared to be the most worried.

'What the hell am I goin' to do with all this lot?' he demanded as Caleb reined his team to a halt in front of the sheriff's office. 'We just ain't got the facilities.'

'That is not my problem,' grinned Caleb. 'All I am doing is bringing in the bodies of wanted outlaws. All I am interested in now is getting my money.'

The sheriff grunted unhappily. 'I ain't even got nowhere to keep 'em until they're properly identified. I guess the only place is Jake Mansell's undertaker's parlour. That's down the street, I'll show you.' Caleb was happy enough to go along with that and waved Royston and Ben to follow.

Jake Mansell, while on the one hand welcoming the business, was rather more concerned with who was going to pay his bill. The town council normally paid in the case of one or even two strangers dying in the town, but the mayor had made it very plain that they were not prepared to pay for so many. In the end Caleb volunteered to pay for it all, up to a maximum of $100. This amount seemed to please the undertaker and he opened up his parlour.

Gus Spencer was taken round to Doc Philips who looked at the wounds and pronounced that had Gus been a cow he would have had little choice but to slaughter him. However, when Caleb produced a ten-dollar note he seemed quite certain that he would be able to do something, remarking that people and animals were not that different when it came to mending broken bones and stitching cuts.

After the bodies had been taken into the undertaker's parlour and Gus found a bed in Doc Philips's house, Royston and Ben decided that they were ravenously hungry and took themselves off to Alma's Eatin' House. Caleb was about to join them when he was suddenly accosted by Mrs Bluebell White and Mrs DuPétin.

'Reverend!' began Mrs DuPétin. 'I have just been witness to a spectacle the likes of which I have no desire to ever witness again. I...that is we...the women of Rose Creek, have no doubt that you are what you claim to be, a properly ordained minister of religion, but we nevertheless find it most peculiar, not to say almost abhorrent, that any man of the church should be involved in the murder of fellow men, no matter what those men may have done.'

'I look upon it as doing God's work,' smiled Caleb. 'Nearly all those men were guilty of either murder or rape or at least robbery. I know God is all powerful, but I also know that He has called on me to help Him tidy up a few loose ends since He has far more important matters to attend.' This reply seemed to silence Mrs DuPétin for a few moments and Caleb decided to argue further. 'It isn't really all that much different to you once being a slave owner. Did God give you the right to treat your fellow men in such a way?'

'That was different!' she huffed. 'They were black and I was white; it was more natural for white folk to have slaves.'

'Did you ever ask the black folk what they thought?' smiled Caleb. 'Anyhow, I did promise to undertake certain tasks and services when I returned. Do you still want me?'

'It just doesn't seem right having a preacher who thinks nothing of killing other men!' complained Mrs DuPétin.

'I have known certain white ministers who have raped slaves and even one or two who have beaten slaves to death,' said Caleb. 'Would they be just as unacceptable or is it because of my colour as well as what I do?'

Mrs White suddenly spoke up. 'I must confess that opinion is somewhat divided on both issues,' she said, 'but the vast majority are in favour of having you perform those functions which can only properly be undertaken by an ordained minister, and I think I speak for Mrs DuPétin on this as well.' The lady in question scowled but nodded slightly.

Caleb smiled and nodded. 'I believe I did ask you to prepare the church.'

'It is being cleaned out even now,' said Mrs White.

'Good,' said Caleb. 'Now, ladies, if you don't mind I am very hungry. I haven't eaten a decent meal in what seems like days and a large steak at Alma's is beckoning.' Once again Mrs DuPétin scowled and Mrs White smiled and Caleb doffed his hat and left them.

The steak at Alma's was up to the high standard Caleb had expected but this time he was surrounded by a crowd of curious onlookers, mostly children but including quite a few adults who appeared to treat the occasion as they would the odd travelling shows which had strange and exotic animals. The experience was not new to Caleb although Royston and Ben found it all rather unnerving and did not finish their meal. Afterwards most of the crowd insisted on following Caleb wherever he went including the privy where one adult and three little boys simply stood and stared as he performed his normal bodily functions. He remembered making some comment about his functions being the same as anyone else's and of the same colour but it did not seem to have any effect upon the man.

When he returned to the sheriff's office some time later, he found that an inventory of the dead outlaws had been drawn up and all their weapons collected and piled in the office. The normal practice was for guns, ammunition, saddles and saddle-bags to become the property of the bounty hunter.

'I suppose the best thing I can do with all that lot,' said Caleb referring to the guns and assortment of saddlery, 'is see what I can get for them down at the livery stable and the gunsmiths. In fact I think I'll give the lot to Royston and Ben, they can have whatever they fetch. What about the outlaws?'

'Eighteen thousand five hundred and fifty dollars!' declared the sheriff. 'That's in addition to the four thousand you've already got comin' for Smith, Sanchez, Gray and Taylor. Almost twenty-three thousand dollars! Man, that's more money than I could ever earn in my whole life!'

'It isn't all mine,' said Caleb. 'I've promised some to Royston and Ben and I have to give some to Gus Spencer, he's going to need it.'

'What you do with it is up to you,' grumbled the sheriff. 'It just seems like I'm at the wrong end of the business.'

'That's your choice,' reminded Caleb. 'How soon do I get the money?'

'All bein' well, you should be able to draw it from the bank on Monday, maybe

Tuesday. I've already checked with the bank and they can cover it, all I need is the OK from the State Justice Department.'

'I guess I can wait,' grinned Caleb. 'It looks like I've got plenty to do in Rose Creek for a while, even if Mrs DuPétin isn't too sure.'

'You're the wrong colour as far as she's concerned,' said the sheriff. 'She likes to make herself heard and likes to think that she is the most important person in town but she always ends up going along with the majority. It's been a couple of years at least since we had us a minister in Rose Creek. It'd've been excitin' enough had you been a normal preacher but you bein' what you are is sure to bring in all the folk from the outlyin' farms an' ranches. Yes, sir, I'm fully expectin' Sunday to be just about the busiest day this town has ever known.'

'I hope they all behave themselves,' smiled Caleb. Satisfied that all that could be done was being done. He returned to the street where the crowd of the curious had, if anything, increased in size and went along to Doc Philips's house.

'Have you got anything to get rid of unwanted parasites?' he asked as Doc Philips invited him in. At first the doc did not understand what he meant but he eventually understood.

'You have to remember that since you have been in Rose Creek there's been more happening in one week than in the last ten years,' said the veterinarian. 'Give them a couple of days and they'll be back to normal.'

'I hope so,' nodded Caleb. 'How's Gus and can you do anything to help him?'

Doc Philips shook his head sadly. 'I can mend the broken ribs, I've had to do that often enough, but I just don't have the skills to save his leg. All I can do is take it off and I'm not too sure about doing that. Veterinarians don't normally have to amputate limbs, the animal is usually put down but I don't think anyone would appreciate it if I just put a bullet through his brain.'

'There's nobody else who can do it,' said Caleb. 'You'll just have to do your best.

At least it will give you some experience in amputating legs.'

'I'll do my best but I'm not promising that he'll even survive the operation. The point is it's got to come off pretty damned soon and by soon I mean today.'

'Is there anything I can do?' asked Caleb.

'The best thing you can do is go along to the saloon and buy a couple of bottles of whiskey,' replied the doc.

'Two bottles?' queried Caleb.

'Yes, two,' grinned the doc. 'One for him and one for me!'

'Can I see him?' asked Caleb.

'Sure, why not?' said the doc. 'It might be a good idea to let him know what's got to happen.'

'I'll tell him,' promised Caleb. He was shown into the small back bedroom where Gus lay looking a lot better than he had but which was due primarily to having been cleaned up. He smiled weakly at the preacher.

'I guess I owe you one,' he croaked. 'I expected you to leave me up there to die or even help me on my way with a bullet through my head.'

'Would you have done that to me?' asked Caleb. Gus plainly had great difficulty in hearing what Caleb said and the question had to be repeated much louder.

'Nothin' more certain!' said Gus managing a weak grin. Caleb was not quite certain if Gus meant that or not.

'Anyhow, you're here now,' said Caleb very loudly and close to Gus's ear. 'Between us we managed to get all the outlaws. Eighteen thousand dollars, not a bad few days' work.'

Once again Gus managed a weak smile. 'I guess it cost me pretty dear. The doc thought I was unconscious but even if I can't hear too well, I know he intends to take my leg off.'

Caleb nodded. 'There's nothing else he can do,' he confirmed. 'He wants to do it today. I'm just going to the saloon for a bottle of whiskey. You're going to need it if you don't want to feel anything.'

Gus nodded. 'I saw a man's leg bein' taken off once, he had drunk almost a whole bottle of whiskey and he didn't seem to feel anythin'. I know the doctor had that leg off in about ten seconds flat; I ain't never seen a man work so fast.' Caleb hoped that the veterinarian would be as quick.

Caleb in fact bought three bottles of whiskey, one for himself since despite his apparent hard exterior, he was really quite squeamish when it came to operating on people. Gus needed little encouragement to drink the whiskey and long before he had reached halfway, it was obvious that he was very drunk. Caleb too had a couple of long draws on his bottle but he was pleased to note that Doc Philips did not have any. The only place the operation could be carried out was in the kitchen on Mrs Philips's kitchen table and whilst it was plain that she was not too happy about it, she did not raise any objections and even helped her husband during the procedure.

In actual fact the process took less than thirty seconds before the stump of Gus's leg above where the knee had been was being sewn up. A few minutes later it was securely bound and Gus was returned to his bed and Mrs Philips was giving her kitchen table a thorough scrubbing. The offending limb was destroyed inside the pot-bellied stove in the kitchen.

For the next few days Caleb was kept fully occupied performing christenings, marriages and even one funeral. He took three separate church services, taking the opportunity at the one big service on Sunday morning to form his sermon around the Old Testament teaching of an eye for an eye, all the time keeping his eyes firmly fixed on Mrs DuPétin in the front row.

Clearance for his bounty money came through on the Monday morning and immediately Royston and Ben were demanding their share. Caleb relented a little and gave them $1,500 dollars each, plus whatever they could get from the sale of all the outlaws' belongings including horses. They succeeded in raising another $1,000 this way, although Caleb knew that had they persisted they could have raised another $500 but they seemed more than satisfied and Caleb was well aware that it would not be that long before it was all either lost, stolen or wasted on drink and women.

After giving Royston and Ben their money, Caleb was left with $15,500 plus the $4,000 he had earned earlier. He did toy briefly with the idea of simply riding out and leaving Gus Spencer to fend for himself, but after giving the matter some thought and after paying out all the monies he had promised for the burial of the outlaws and Gus's treatment and in the light of Gus apparently making a good recovery, he relented and made arrangements with the president of the bank for Gus to be paid $7,000. The remainder he pocketed and promised himself that this time he was going to save most of it instead of giving it all away, which was what usually happened. Time alone would tell if this idea ever materialized.

For his part Gus appeared more than grateful for what Caleb proposed and had apparently decided that he was going to settle in Rose Creek since he had taken a fancy to Doc Philips's daughter and she, apparently, to him. The $7,000 would be more than enough to set them both up and possibly buy the general store which was open to offers. Royston and Ben had already started to make inroads into their money, the colour of their skin seeming suddenly unimportant to the girls in the saloon and to almost everyone else in Rose Creek. Caleb did attempt to make the pair see some sense but he eventually gave up and watched them slowly get rid of their money.

Caleb was urged to stay on as permanent minister of Rose Creek, but he did not feel quite ready to commit himself to such a steady lifestyle as yet. He did stay on another week and undertook various duties and services but, at the end of that week he was quite adamant and, to save any arguments or pleadings, he decided to leave during the night.

Dawn found him at least thirty miles away from Rose Creek and studying two men huddled around a fire some distance below him. If they were who he thought they were, there was another $2,000 going begging....

This Large Print Book for the Partially sighted, who cannot read normal print, is published under the auspices of

THE ULVERSCROFT FOUNDATION

THE ULVERSCROFT FOUNDATION

. . . we hope that you have enjoyed this Large Print Book. Please think for a moment about those people who have worse eyesight problems than you . . . and are unable to even read or enjoy Large Print, without great difficulty.

You can help them by sending a donation, large or small to:

**The Ulverscroft Foundation,
1, The Green, Bradgate Road,
Anstey, Leicestershire, LE7 7FU,
England.**

or request a copy of our brochure for more details.

The Foundation will use all your help to assist those people who are handicapped by various sight problems and need special attention.

Thank you very much for your help.